Nashville Midwives

The midwives of Music City!

Welcome to Nashville, Tennessee! The home of country music *and* Skylar, Brianna and Lori. Midwives at Legacy Women's Clinic, they dedicate their days and nights to their patients. But when Skylar, Brianna and Lori aren't helping to bring bundles of joy into the world, they are facing meet-cutes with colleagues that leave hearts racing! Will their love stories be so magical they could inspire the city's next big country star as they sing their latest hit on the Bluebird Café's stage...?

Find out in...

Skylar and Jared's story
Unbuttoning the Bachelor Doc

and

Brianna and Knox's story
The Rebel Doctor's Secret Child

Available now!

And don't miss...

Lori and Zac's story

Coming soon!

Dear Reader,

Welcome back to Nashville, home of the Grand Ole Opry, Goo Goo Clusters and many country music hopefuls. A lot is about to change at Nashville's Legacy Clinic. You see, our midwife in training, Brianna Rogers, has a secret she hasn't shared with anyone, not even her new friends Lori and Sky. While Dr. Knox Collins, son of country music stars Gail and Charlie Collins, is only at the Legacy Clinic temporarily, he's sure the midwife is hiding something and he's determined to find out exactly what it is. But is Nashville's former bad boy ready for the secret that will change not only his and Bree's lives, but also the life of her eight-year-old niece?

Sit back, kick off your boots and hold on while our rebel doc and our mysterious midwife go on a wild, wild ride that can only end when they finally find the happily-ever-after they both deserve.

Happy reading,

Deanne Anders

THE REBEL DOCTOR'S SECRET CHILD

DEANNE ANDERS

MEDICAL ROMANCE

Harlequin®
MEDICAL ROMANCE

Recycling programs for this product may not exist in your area.

ISBN-13: 978-1-335-94265-4

The Rebel Doctor's Secret Child

Harlequin Enterprises ULC
22 Adelaide St. West, 41st Floor
Toronto, Ontario M5H 4E3, Canada
www.Harlequin.com

Printed in U.S.A.

Deanne Anders was reading romance while her friends were still reading Nancy Drew, and she knew she'd hit the jackpot when she found a shelf of Harlequin Presents books in her local library. Years later she discovered the fun of writing her own. Deanne lives in Florida with her husband and their spoiled Pomeranian. During the day she works as a nursing supervisor. With her love of everything medical and romance, writing for Harlequin Medical Romance is a dream come true.

Books by Deanne Anders

Harlequin Medical Romance

The Surgeon's Baby Bombshell
Stolen Kiss with the Single Mom
Sarah and the Single Dad
The Neurosurgeon's Unexpected Family
December Reunion in Central Park
Florida Fling with the Single Dad
Pregnant with the Secret Prince's Babies
Flight Nurse's Florida Fairy Tale
A Surgeon's Christmas Baby

Nashville Midwives

Unbuttoning the Bachelor Doc

Visit the Author Profile page at Harlequin.com.

This book is dedicated to all the medical staff
that volunteer their time at our local clinics,
schools and with our local disaster teams.
Thank you for your service.

PROLOGUE

EXCITEMENT VIBRATED THROUGH Brianna Rogers as she followed the office manager, Sable, into the crowded conference room. With her arms loaded down with boxes of donuts, Brianna looked across the table at all the people she'd soon be working with. She'd done it. In just a few months, she'd be working as a certified nurse midwife. The opportunity for a residency at Nashville's Women's Legacy Clinic was one that she'd never imagined receiving. It was known as the premier women's clinic in the city, so the experience she'd receive here would be priceless.

As the door opened and a silver-haired man with kind blue eyes came in, the room went quiet. Bree rushed to her seat. She had only met the founder of the clinic, Dr. Jack Warner, once during an interview, but she admired the practice he'd built and especially the home for pregnant women in need of a safe place to stay that he had founded.

He took his seat at the end of the table then reached for the tablet Sable had told her contained the itinerary for the meeting.

"First off, I'd like to welcome two new colleagues. I hope you've all met our new resident midwife, Brianna Rogers. She's a recent graduate of Vanderbilt and came to us highly recommended."

A man yelled, "Go Commodores," from across the room, taking the attention off her, something she appreciated. One of the midwives, Sky, waved at her from down the table. Bree waved back. Even with the unwanted attention, she was already feeling at home here.

"Also, I want you to welcome Dr. Knox Collins, who will be filling in for Dr. Hennison, who, I'm sure you all know, just welcomed another baby boy."

Bree's heart skipped a beat and her arms and face prickled with tiny pinpricks. No. It was impossible that he could be there. A roaring in her ears started as her eyes scanned the room, stopping when she saw a man with laughing gray eyes and a devilish smile that should have come with a warning.

Never in her wildest dreams would she have

imagined herself stuck looking across the table at the man who had broken her sister's heart and left Bree to pick up the pieces. Especially since one of those pieces had been a newborn baby. She'd never forget the first time she'd heard that name. It had been when her phone rang. She hadn't spoken to her sister in months and was so happy to see her name on the display.

Suddenly, she was back there, eight years earlier. Brittany, her voice overflowing with a happiness Bree hadn't heart in years, laughing as she told Bree the news. "It's a girl, Bree. A beautiful baby girl. I have a daughter. You're an aunt."

Stunned, Bree didn't know what to say. Brittany had been pregnant? How was that possible without Bree knowing about it?

"Well, aren't you going to congratulate me?" her sister asked.

"Of course," Bree said, recovering from the shock of her sister's words. "Where are you?"

Bree listened closely as her sister explained how she'd gone into labor early and the baby was still in the hospital.

"Who's the father?" Bree asked, unable to hold back the question any longer. Brittany had been known to hook up with some less than desirable types in the past.

"It's Knox Collins, Gail and Charles Collins's son. But you can't tell anyone. Me. This baby. We mean nothing to him. He's messed up, Bree. He drinks and parties all the time. I don't want that for my daughter. Promise me you won't tell anyone, Bree. Promise me."

Bree had no choice but to agree. If Brittany thought the man would be a bad influence on her daughter, she had no choice but to believe her. She'd ask for more information the next time her sister called her.

But the next call she received wasn't from her sister. Instead, it was from the hospital. She could hear the woman's voice. "I'm sorry, Ms. Rogers, but there's been a terrible accident."

She told the woman that she was wrong. She'd just spoken with her sister only hours earlier. Her sister couldn't be gone.

She remembered holding her niece in her arms for the first time, knowing it should have been Brittany standing there to take her baby home. Not Bree.

Overwhelming grief had threatened to overtake her then, but she pushed it back. Just like she had when she'd realized she was suddenly responsible for her sister's newborn baby. There was no time for grieving. Because if she let it take hold of her, she'd never climb out of the dark pit of it. She'd never be able to take care of the child who had no one else. Just like Bree had no one else but that child.

The noise of the room rose, bringing her back to reality as everyone around her stood up to leave.

Looking down the table she saw Knox accepting the greetings from the clinic's staff. How was it that he stood there, smiling and happy, going on with his life while her sister's life was cut so short?

Bree shook her head. No. She wouldn't let herself go there. Ally had to be her first priority. The little girl had given Bree a reason to keep on going for years now, to keep pushing to better herself so that she could provide a good life for her niece. And there was no way she was going to let some hotshot rebel doc like Knox Collins get in her way.

CHAPTER ONE

BRIANNA ROGERS WAS trying to ignore them. All of them. The giggling nurse with bouncy honey-blond curls Bree would give her already strained credit card to have, the anesthesia nurse whose toothpaste-ad smile could blind someone, and the drooling surgical tech whose no-nonsense attitude had turned disgustingly mushy. But most of all, she was trying to ignore the man in the middle of all three of them, Knox Collins.

From the moment Bree had attended her first staff meeting at Women's Legacy Clinic, she'd made it her priority to avoid Knox. For three months she had accomplished the impossible by managing to dodge the man whom she'd considered enemy number one for the past eight years. It looked like her luck had run out now, and the only thing she could do was pretend that he wasn't there.

Her teeth ground against each other when

the blonde nurse giggled again at something Knox had said. She forced her eyes back to the computer screen in front of her and did her best to block out everyone else in the room.

Should she have turned down the opportunity that Dr. Warner, Jack, had given her when she'd found out Nashville's own bad boy turned doctor was going to be there? Maybe, but how could she? With the amount of student loans she had and the cost of raising her niece, she was lucky to get the chance to do her midwife residency at the clinic. There was no way she could afford to turn down the opportunity. Not having to leave Nashville or change her niece's school had been a blessing and reduced the stress that always seemed to be right around the corner waiting to overwhelm her. Oh, she'd been tempted to pack up Ally and skedaddle out of town, but where would she go? It would have taken months to get set up with another clinic. Months of falling further and further behind financially.

So instead, she'd convinced herself that if she was careful and kept her head down, she'd be able to avoid Dr. Knox Collins. And it had worked. Until now.

"Need some help?" A deep voice came from right behind her, causing her to jump then grab for the coffee mug as her hand knocked against its side.

"What?" she asked, the word ending with a squeak that made her sound like the mouse her sister had always accused her of being. Looking around, she saw that the other staff members had finally left the room. Clearing her throat, she tried again. "I'm sorry, do you need something, Dr. Collins?"

"I just noticed you staring at the screen," he said, his hand waving toward her computer, "and I wondered if you needed help charting something in the delivery record. One of the nurses was just telling me that it was a difficult delivery you and Lori just attended. Sometimes that complicates the charting."

It had been a difficult delivery with the baby being much larger than expected and its face turned up. It had taken everyone working together to get him out. But with Lori, her midwife preceptor beside her, Bree had been in control of the situation. "No. There's no problem."

"Good. I know Lori's your preceptor, but if there's anything I can do, or anything you have a question about, just ask. I know I'm just here temporarily, but I want to help if I can," Knox said before moving back to his own computer.

Once he wasn't looking over her shoulder, Bree's body relaxed, at least a little. He was still too close and his words just made things worse. Because the biggest surprise she'd had since the day they'd first met was that Dr. Knox Collins didn't seem like the coldhearted, self-absorbed man that her sister had made him out to be. He seemed to be truly interested in the patients and the staff at the clinic.

Or was the overly nice doctor he presented to the staff just an act to make people like him? Didn't the man ever wear something besides a smile on his face? Didn't he ever have a bad day? Maybe if you were the only son of mega-rich country music stars you didn't have bad days.

But no matter how nice the man appeared to be, she had to keep her defenses up around him. The last thing she needed was to have him focus that charm of his on her.

"Why? Do you need more members in your fan club?" she asked, the sarcasm as thick as the butter on a country biscuit.

Had she really just said that?

Way to keep yourself off his radar, Bree.

"I keep getting the feeling that you have something against me. Do you want to talk about it? Clear the air? Is there something I did?" Knox said, the sincerity in his voice setting her teeth to grinding again. Didn't the man ever get mad?

And what would he say if she told him it was definitely something he'd done? He'd gotten her sister pregnant and then ignored her. Bree couldn't blame him for her sister's death—that had been the result of her sister taking a curve around a mountain too fast—but that didn't mean Bree could forgive him for his part in her sister's last days. For not being a man her sister wanted to help raise her daughter.

She knew she couldn't say any of this. Not if she wanted to keep her promise to her sister. And not if she wanted to protect her niece. Instead, she had to find a way to put some distance between them.

"I'm sorry, Dr. Knox. I appreciate your offer to help. It's just been a long day."

The silence in the room was deafening. She knew he wasn't buying her excuse. She'd spent the past three months avoiding him and apparently he had noticed. Had she been that transparent?

"Hey guys, what's up?" Lori asked as she entered the room. Bree released a slow, steadying breath. She'd known from day one that she and Lori were going to make a good team. Though only a few years older than she was, Lori had been with the practice since she had obtained her midwifery certification. She'd taken Bree in as if they'd been friends for a lifetime, and she shared all her experience and knowledge. Lori was someone people knew they could trust the moment they met her. More than once, Bree had started to spill all her secrets with the midwife.

"I'm almost finished with the charting if you want to look it over," Bree said, turning toward the doorway, glad to end the conversation with Knox.

"Sure," Lori said, looking between the two of them, her eyes seeing more than what Bree wanted her to see. Her preceptor was smart and observant.

"I heard that the two of you had a challenging delivery," Knox said, turning his attention to Lori.

"Posterior delivery, but Bree handled it perfectly," Lori said as she took a seat next to Bree. "She's going to make a great midwife."

"I was just telling her that the staff was saying she did great today," Knox said.

"She did," Lori said. "I'm very proud of her." Bree ducked her head as her cheeks warmed with a blush that would make the freckles on her nose stand out even more.

Where her sister had thrived on the applause and praises of the press and audiences when they were young, it had always made Bree feel uncomfortable and awkward to have others compliment her. It was one of many reasons she had protested when her sister and their agent had decided it was time to take their duet to the next level in the country music scene.

"I still have a lot to learn," Bree said, making herself lift her eyes and look at her coworkers.

"Dr. Collins, they're ready for you in the OR," Kelly, the nurse who'd been giggling with Knox's group earlier, said from the open doorway.

Once Knox left the room, Bree could feel Lori's eyes on her. "What was that about?"

"What?" Bree asked, pretending not to know what Lori was referring to. Unable to hold Lori's gaze, Bree looked back at the computer screen, pretending to study it.

"There was something going on between the two of you. I could feel it."

"It was nothing." All Bree wanted to do was finish her charting and get out of the room before Knox returned.

But the experienced midwife was not going

to let it go. Reaching over, Lori shut the door. "I might believe that if this was the first time I'd noticed the change in you when Dr. Collins was around. Has he done something? Anything to make you uncomfortable?"

It seemed that would be the theme of the day. She was too tired to go through another review of all the things Knox had done again.

Still, she knew Lori was concerned that he had done something inappropriate, and Bree couldn't let her think that. "No. He's been nothing but helpful to me since I came to the practice."

"So, what is it, then? I know we were all worried that he'd be this stuck-up rich kid, but I haven't found him to be that way at all."

Neither had Bree, which had thrown her off, leaving her feeling a guilt that she hadn't expected. Which led her back to the possibility that the man might have truly changed. What if he wasn't the selfish, ego-obsessed man Bree had assumed from her sister's description? And even worse, what if he had never been that man?

No. She wouldn't even consider such a thing. Brittany might not have always been up-front when it came to getting what she wanted, but she never would have made Bree promise to keep her daughter away from her father if she hadn't had a good reason for it. Bree, herself, had looked into his background after Brittany had called her and told her about the baby. Knox Collins had been a troubled teenager who'd been kicked out of more than one private academy. Reports of his partying his way through college were all over the local media.

"Of course, if it's something more personal, I wouldn't blame you. The man is certainly nice to look at. I think half the staff is in lust with him." Lori gave Bree a wicked smile. "It's nothing to be embarrassed about. He's not my type, but I get it."

Bree looked over at Lori. The midwife had a natural beauty that came from her generous smile and kind eyes. "What is your type?"

"I'm not quite sure," Lori said, her eyes looking off into space before returning to Bree. "I'm stuck somewhere between wanting a Mr. Darcy and a Jamie Fraser."

Bree hadn't ever cared much for Mr. Darcy, too stuffy, but she had watched every season of *Outlander* and couldn't help but think that Knox, with his thick light brown curls that fell almost to his shoulders, would make a great Jamie Fraser.

"Really, Lori, there's nothing like that going

on." No matter how good-looking the man was, she would never let herself be attracted to him.

Lori studied her a little too long before finally shaking her head. "Okay, but if there is something that's bothering you, I want you to know you can talk to me. No matter what it's about, but especially if it's something that could affect your work."

Bree bit back words that would spill the secret she had worked so hard to keep for the past eight years. She trusted Lori, she did, but there was too much at stake. If the truth came out about who was Ally's father, Bree could lose the child she loved as her own. Let the other midwife think that Bree was harboring some deep longing for Dr. Collins. Better that than she know the truth.

"If you're good, then, I'm going to let you finish up rounds. We don't have any new labor patients, but there is a day-two postpartum on the floor who needs discharge orders put in. You remember Kristina? It's her third baby. No complications. Just look in on her and make sure she doesn't need anything before discharge. You can meet me back at the office when you're finished."

As soon as Lori had shut the door to the physician's work room, Bree dropped her head to the desk. Why did life have to be so complicated? It had always been her sister who had loved drama. Not Bree. She took in a big breath then let it out, along with all the pent-up stress of the past few minutes, and made herself look on the bright side of things. Dr. Collins had only a few more weeks before his ad-locum contract would be finished and he'd be moving on.

She'd managed for weeks to keep her head down around him. And if luck was on her side, she'd be able to continue to avoid him. But then again, when had luck been on her side?

"I'm not sure I understand," Knox repeated for the third time. "I thought Lori was Bree's preceptor," he said to Dr. Warner.

"I'll still be her preceptor," Lori interjected. "I just think that it would be a good thing for her to get an opportunity to do some work in the county women's clinic. You've been saying you need more volunteers to help. This will work out perfectly," Lori said.

There was something about the way that Lori was looking at him that set his warning bells ringing. It reminded him of the look his momma got when she was about to set him up with her newest matchmaking victim.

"Lori's right," Dr. Warner said as he looked at the two of them from across his desk. "Brianna needs to get some experience in a women's clinic like the one run by the county. There is no telling where she might find herself in the future. Our clinic is lucky enough to have fancy equipment with all the bells and whistles. If she ends up in one of the more rural parts of our state, she might not have those."

Jack was right. The older man had built Legacy Women's Clinic into one of the best clinics in the state during his career. And though he'd stepped back and let his son take over a lot of the running of the clinic now, Knox respected the man and couldn't deny that Jack wanted only the best for all his staff. Unfortunately, that meant Knox was going to have to agree with him. With the shortage of obstetricians nationwide and the rural areas of Tennessee depending on the certified midwives to fill in where they could, Bree would be welcomed in one of the rural areas.

"Okay. Fine. I'll work with her. But I need to know her proficiencies as well as her weaknesses. I don't want to put her in a position she's not comfortable with." It was bad enough that she seemed to have taken to immediately disliking him, something that he still didn't understand. There was even the possibility that Bree would refuse to work with him.

There was a soft knock on the door before Bree stuck her head inside. "You wanted to see me?"

Knox could see the hesitancy in her expression as she entered the room and looked around. When her eyes met his, all the color drained from her face. At that moment she looked so young with her strawberry blond hair pulled back in a tight braid that was a little lopsided. There was an innocence in her green eyes that sparked a sudden, unexpected need to protect her. Just how innocent was she? He hadn't missed the fact that she'd actually blushed when Lori had complimented her earlier that day. When had he ever seen a woman do that? Had he ever?

His attitude concerning Jack and Lori's request to allow the young midwife to work with him at the county clinic made a U-turn. Bree needed to get out into the real world. It had certainly been an eye-opener for him. And one that had changed his whole career. It would be interesting to watch her interact with the women he saw there. Women who didn't have the resources for the kind of care they received at Legacy. Women down on their luck and needing help.

"Come in, Brianna," Jack said, then waved her to the seat next to Knox. "We were just discussing with Dr. Collins the possibility of you helping him out at the county clinic for a few hours a week."

Knox wouldn't have thought her face could have gone any whiter, but it did. For a moment she just stared at Jack, then she turned to Lori. "Is there a problem with me working with you?"

"No, not at all," Lori reassured her. "You are doing beyond what I could have hoped for at this stage of your training. But Jack and I think that you could be an asset to the county clinic while increasing your experience. Here we have a controlled atmosphere where we see our patients on a schedule so we can prepare for our day. At the clinic, you will see more of a variety of patients, including more gynecology patients. It's also something that will look good on your résumé. More importantly, you'll be helping women who need your care."

"I've helped out at Legacy House when I've had the time," Bree said. "And I have…other responsibilities. I don't have a lot of free hours."

"We wouldn't expect you to work any more

hours. If Dr. Collins agrees to this, you'll be able to get your clinic hours at the county two days each week in exchange for two days in the clinic here."

When they all turned toward him, Knox felt the tension in the room soar. While Jack's eyes seemed confident that Knox would agree, and Lori had one eyebrow lifted in challenge, Bree's eyes were round as saucers with a fear he could not understand. Had he somehow intimidated her? Was that what all this tension he felt around her was all about? No, the comments she'd made that morning, ones he'd chosen to ignore, showed that she wasn't afraid to speak her mind with him.

Maybe it was because of who his parents were. That, he was used to. A lot of people were overly impressed by his parents' fame. But somehow he knew that wasn't it, either. This was something different. And for some irrational reason, while it should have irritated him, it intrigued him. He wanted to know what it was that had her bristling every time he came into the room.

"I think it would be a great learning experience for Bree, and I could certainly use the help," he said. Neither of those statements was a lie. The clinic was chronically short on staff.

He was only filling in for a friend for a few weeks, but he could use the help, even if it was temporary.

Then Bree did something he wasn't expecting. She pulled back her shoulders and sent all of them a confident, though a little wobbly, smile. "Okay, then. It's settled. I look forward to working with Dr. Collins at the county clinic."

The tremble of her lips as she said the words betrayed that she did everything but look forward to the next month of the two of them working together. Was he the only one in the room who could see she was most definitely not excited about working with him at all? From the smiles on Lori's and Jack's faces, he was afraid that he was.

It had been a long time since he'd had this amount of interest in a woman. Bree Rogers was a mystery, one that he couldn't wait to solve.

"Is this about this morning?" Bree asked as soon as she and Lori were alone in Lori's office.

"Of course not," Lori said and then sighed. "Okay, maybe a little. The truth is Jack mentioned the idea to me and I thought it might be good for you to take this opportunity, not just to learn more about how to work in a county clinic, but also to learn to work with coworkers that you might not like."

"I don't not like Dr. Collins. I just don't…" She'd talked herself into a corner now. How did she explain to Lori her feelings for Knox without spilling all her secrets? "I don't find him particularly likeable."

Lori rolled her eyes at Bree's contradictory statement. "Like I said, Jack—Dr. Warner— came up with this idea. To be honest, I think there's a possibility he has heard some of the office chatter suggesting that you have a problem with Knox. I'm not the only one who has noticed how you have a habit of avoiding our ad-locum doc."

She should have known she couldn't keep her feelings toward the doctor hidden in such a tight-knit group as the one that worked at Legacy Clinic. Did that mean they were talking about her behind her back? Did they, like Lori had, think she had some schoolgirl crush on him?

"Look at it this way. There's only a few more weeks to Dr. Collins's contract here. Do a good job and learn everything you can at the clinic. He's a good doctor. You might be surprised how much he can teach you. He might not have been a doctor for very long, but he's worked some places so far back in the mountains that the nearest hospital was over an hour's drive away."

Bree had heard that Knox had even done some work off the grid up in the Smoky Mountains, which in spite of herself she wanted to hear more about. And like Lori had reminded her, Knox's contract would be over soon and he would be moving on. She just had to hold it together till then. She'd kept her sister's secret for eight years. She could do it a few more weeks.

That thought had her feeling better, until a few hours later when she arrived to pick Ally up from her after-school care program. Seeing her little girl surrounded by her friends as they worked on a craft project made all her protective instincts kick in. Just eight years old, Ally was already showing signs of being a people magnet like her mother. Unlike Bree, who'd been shy most of her childhood, her sister Brittany had always had a way with people. Ally's friendly smile and quick laughter helped her make friends wherever she went. She was sweet and innocent and Bree would protect that little girl with the last breath in her body.

She would never allow the man whom her sister didn't approve of take Ally away from her. Never.

"How was your day? Did you deliver any babies?" Ally asked.

Bree flipped a pancake over before turning to her niece. The last thing she wanted to do was talk about her day, but she couldn't ignore the question.

When Ally had started school and Bree had her own classes along with two jobs sometimes, it had become hard for Bree to spend the quality time she wanted to with Ally. Most nights dinner had become fast food or boxed mac-'n'-cheese, so Bree made the effort to make the middle of the week meal fun and a chance for the two of them to spend time together. Since Ally's favorite meal was breakfast, Bree had deemed Wednesday night as breakfast night.

"I did deliver a baby. A really big one with adorable chubby cheeks." Bree turned around and puffed her cheeks out, making a face that had Ally laughing. "What about you? Did the teacher like the picture you drew?"

Ally's laughter stopped and her eyes filled with tears.

"What's wrong? Did something happen to

the picture?" While Ally's picture, one that showed Bree and Ally in front of the small house Bree rented, wouldn't have won any awards, she had worked hard on it, and Bree knew Ally's teacher had to have seen that.

"Holly asked me why I didn't have a mommy or daddy," Ally said, before wiping her eyes with her shirtsleeve.

This wasn't the first time someone in Ally's class had asked her that question. Bree had struggled with the decision of whether to tell Ally about her mother or whether to let her grow up believing that Bree was her mother. To Bree, Ally had been her little girl from the moment the nurse had put her in her arms.

Still, no matter how much Bree loved Ally as her own, it was important that she knew about her mother. In some ways, Ally helped to keep her sister's memory alive for both of them.

Bree knew grief. She and Brittany had lost their parents within a few months of each other. It had been hard, but she'd still had her sister. They'd shared everything from a womb to a room for the first eighteen years of their lives. Not having her sister left a hole that ate at Bree. It was only in the middle of the night, after Ally was safely tucked into bed, that Bree allowed herself to let the grief of losing her sister take over. But the next morning, she pasted on a smile and went back to living, for her sister as much as for her niece.

After taking the pancake from the griddle, Bree went around the island and hugged the little girl. "I'm sorry. I know it makes you sad when someone asks you questions about your mommy."

As always, she avoided the question of Ally's daddy, something she knew she wouldn't be able to do for too much longer. Till now Ally had been satisfied with Bree's explanation that there had been an accident that had taken her mother away, but it was only a matter of time till the child became more curious about her father. And what was Bree going to do then? She'd found it hard each time she had to explain to Ally how her mother had died; explaining that her father hadn't been in the picture when she'd been born would be even harder.

Ally snuggled closer against her and Bree's arms tightened around her small frame.

For now, all Bree could do was give Ally all the love she had and hope it would be enough to shield her from that and all the other heartbreaks she was bound to encounter. Bree knew she'd always appreciated having her parents to lean on when she'd faced her own heartaches.

Of course, that was before the cancer had taken her momma and the bottle had taken her daddy. And then the search for fame had taken Brittany into a whole different place in life than Bree had wanted to go, taking Brittany completely out of Bree's life.

"How about we eat a bunch of pancakes until our tummy hurts and then we can snuggle up together with a couple books till bedtime?"

"Not schoolbooks?" Ally asked. Bree knew she was remembering the months, no, years, that Bree had spent studying for her nursing degree and then her nurse practitioner and midwifery degrees.

"Not schoolbooks," Bree said, though she did have some community health studying she'd planned to do to start preparing for whatever she might encounter with Knox at the clinic. The more she knew, the fewer questions she'd have to ask him.

But later, after their meal and dishes were done, Bree noticed that Ally wasn't paying attention as she read the little girl one of her favorite wizard books. "Do you want us to read something else?"

"I don't feel much like reading. I thought maybe you could tell me a story about my mom instead?"

Bree wasn't surprised at her request after their discussion earlier that night. Bree had been telling Ally stories about Brittany since she was around three. If Bree added a bit to the stories sometimes, it was always for the little girl's benefit. The truth was there were a couple years when Brittany had cut Bree out of her life, which was something Bree would never tell Ally.

"Well, let's see. Where do you want me to start?" Bree asked, though she already knew the answer.

"Start where you and my mom came to Nashville and sang on stage at the Grand Ole Opry," Ally said, snuggling farther down into her covers. "When the two of you were famous."

Bree laughed. "I don't think the two of us were exactly famous. There just weren't a lot of eleven-year-old twins playing guitar and singing Loretta Lynn songs back then."

"Loretta who?" Ally asked.

"Never mind." She'd hold the history of country music lesson till later. "Okay, so you know we'd won a contest at the county fair and made the papers. And then one morning our momma got a phone call inviting us to come sing a couple songs on stage in Nashville. Of course she agreed, but our daddy thought it was a hoax…"

"A what?" Ally asked.

"It's what they used to call scams. Anyway, he called the Opry and asked to speak with the manager, who told him no, it wasn't a hoax. They had seen the article in the paper and they had invited us. It was a good thing it wasn't a scam, too, because our momma was so excited that she had already left the house to pick us up early from school." Bree could still remember the way her momma's eyes had shined when she'd had the principal pull them out of class to tell them. She didn't think she had ever seen her momma so happy. Then Brittany had squealed loud enough that the teachers had stuck their heads out of their classrooms to see what was going on. Before long, the whole school was caught up in the celebration. No one seemed to notice that Bree wasn't celebrating with them. Not even her mother or her sister.

"Tell me about the dress my momma wore," Ally said.

"I've showed you pictures," Bree said, unable to keep the grumble from her voice. She had hated those dresses with the yards of ruffles and bows. The fact that they had been pink, her sister's favorite color, not hers, had nothing to do with it, either. "It was awful. It had all those ruffles and too much lace. It was way too girly."

Ally giggled. "I think it was pretty."

"So there we were, Saturday night, out on the stage, when Loretta Lynn herself came up to your momma and told her that she was 'just the prettiest thing I ever saw.'"

"But you weren't there because you were sick in the dressing room," Ally said.

It had been one of Bree's most embarrassing moments. She'd been throwing up so hard her eyes had watered, and one of the women who worked backstage had to help her clean herself up before she could go on stage. "No, but my momma told me all about it."

"Then the two of you sang that song about being from the country and one of the people there offered y'all a lot of money to sing for them."

"Something like that." Bree was too young to know anything about the money side, but it was the night they got their first agent. Their first in a long line for the next eight years as Brittany and her parents chased their dream for fame and fortune, despite Bree trying to explain to them that she wanted something different for her life.

"I bet if my momma was here right now she'd be a big star. Then I could draw pictures of the three of us up on stage together." Ally yawned and rolled over on to her side, her eyes closing as the long day caught up with her.

"I bet she would," Bree whispered, though in her heart she wasn't so sure. Bree's and Brittany's thirty seconds of fame had been long gone by the time Brittany had died. Brittany had blamed Bree. It had caused a rift between them that Bree had hoped someday to mend. She liked to think that the two of them were moving toward that after the call she received from Brittany before the car crash.

Bree sat there for a few moments until she was sure that the little girl was asleep, then went to her own room to spend a few hours studying. She had no idea what she might encounter at the county clinic but she was going to be as prepared as possible.

Later, when her eyes refused to read another case study, Bree put her books away and climbed into bed. Somehow, she'd managed to avoid the dreaded conversation about Ally's father once more. But for how long? There was going to come a day when she wouldn't be able to avoid that question. And what was she going to say then? How did she tell a story that she didn't really know herself? All she'd been told by Brittany was that she and Knox had been involved and that he'd left her and had no interest in a child. How did you tell a child that her father hadn't wanted her?

And how did Bree know if that was still the way Knox felt now? Brittany's words had been so cryptic that she wasn't even sure if Brittany had ever told him about the pregnancy. There were so many questions she'd never been able to ask her sister. She was having a hard time believing the man she'd watched interacting with the staff today wouldn't want to know his daughter. And if he did? What would that mean for Ally? For Bree?

Since the moment she'd been told by Dr. Warner and Lori that she would be working with Knox at the clinic, Bree had felt a sense of impending doom. As a midwife, she knew that when a patient felt that way, you never ignored it. There was always some reason, some instinctual knowledge, for that intense feeling that something bad was about to happen.

Even as she slipped into sleep, she acknowledged that everything in her life was about to change and all she could do was ensure that she protected her niece no matter what it cost her. Because after losing everyone else in her family, she would not lose Ally.

CHAPTER TWO

Knox watched as Bree entered the aged county building where the small women's clinic where he was filling in for a friend was located.

"Good morning," he said, startling the young midwife as she reached the top of the first set of stairs that would lead to their second-floor office. She looked up at him with her bright green eyes that he always found appealing. Then there was that long strawberry blond hair and those freckles that dusted her nose. She wasn't striking and she didn't fit the trendy idea of beautiful. What was it about her that kept his mind returning to her over and over again?

He shook his head at his early-morning musings. He'd only had time for one cup of coffee so far and it would take a couple more before he'd be ready for clinic hours.

"I have to say that I'm surprised to find you working at one of the city's free clinics," Bree said as she looked around the worn floors and walls that were in deep need of new paint. She didn't seem to be judging the building as much as she was judging him.

"I ran into a friend from college who works here and he needed some time off. The clinic is only open two days a week. It's not really any different from the work that I do when I'm working up in the mountains. I'd already planned to take the temporary position with Legacy, so why not help him out?"

"I wouldn't think you'd have the time. It almost sounds like you don't do anything but work. Which doesn't make sense."

Knox wasn't surprised by her comment. A lot of people figured that with parents as rich as his, there wasn't any reason for him to work. What they didn't get was that he enjoyed his work. Especially work like he got to do in the rural communities in the mountains. "Both jobs are temporary. And both are very different. You won't see the same clientele here that you've been seeing at the Legacy Clinic. A lot of these women don't have insurance or even money to cover high copays. Some of them don't trust the state health care system. And some of them won't trust you, either. Getting someone to trust you after they've been

let down by the system is a major accomplish-
ment. You'll find trust in short supply here.
You might not even like the work. It can be
very repetitive, mostly yearly exams, medication refills, STD testing, that type of thing. But
I can guarantee that it will open your eyes to
the needs of the community."

"I'm here to learn as much as possible. Dr.
Warner and Lori think this will be good for
my training, and their opinions are important
to me. I've worked in a labor and delivery department with patients from all backgrounds
so that won't be a problem."

This was probably the longest conversation
they'd ever shared. Fortunately for the two of
them, there was none of the sarcasm she'd been
so happy to share with him the week before,
which made him feel better about bringing her
in to help out. Maybe having a week to adjust
to the idea of working with him had been good,
though he still didn't understand what it was
about him that caused her to go on the offen-
sive every time she was around him.

"That's good," Knox said as they headed up
the second set of steps. He liked the fact that
Bree wasn't afraid to stand up and say what
she thought. He'd had too many coworkers who
treated him differently either because he was

a doctor or because of his parents. Bree didn't seem to be impressed by either. "I wanted to show you around the building before we went upstairs to the office since when the doors open I won't have the time. Most of the first story takes care of the county clerk business, but the second floor is mostly used by the health department. At the end of the hall is the children's clinic, which you might need to know to refer some of our patients with children there. And before that, on the right, there is a dentist office and health records departments. There is a substance abuse center across from there. Unfortunately you will need to make referrals there, too."

He watched as she studied the areas he pointed out. When she didn't make any comment, he continued. "Any OB patients get referred out. The health department has a separate program for them."

Turning left, he led her to the set of offices where they'd be working together. The simple block letters that read Women's Clinic was the only thing that set itself apart from the other line of doors down the hall. Opening the door, they were met with the one thing that made the clinic possible, its no-nonsense, but still empathetic, office manager.

"Bree, I'd like you to meet the real boss of this joint, Ms. Lucretia Sweet. Don't be fooled by the name. She's only sweet when she wants to be."

"And I'm certainly not sweet till I get my brew in the morning. Hand it over."

Knox did as he was told and handed the special order coffee to the woman who had won his heart the first day he'd shown up to work there.

"Bree's a midwifery resident at Legacy and is going to be helping for the next few weeks so don't run her off," Knox said. "And if you can show her around while I start a pot of real coffee, I'd appreciate it."

"Me run off good help? Especially when it's free? Not going to happen. Come on in here, Bree. Is that short for Brianna?"

"Yes, ma'am. Brianna Rogers, but please call me Bree."

Knox listened to the women's exchange as he started the coffee in the small corner that also provided snacks and water for their patients. After his first good swallow of the dark-roasted drink, he returned to find Lucretia questioning his resident like a military drill sergeant.

"Have you ever worked in a clinic like this? Because I want you to understand that while we might not agree with some of these women's choices, we treat each one of them as equals."

"I did a rotation in the county jail during my masters in nursing degree. I plan on doing my doctorate dissertation on the need for more women's care in the correctional system."

"I didn't know you were planning on getting your doctorate," Knox said as he leaned against the doorjamb and studied the woman. She was gutsy and driven. He liked that. She'd do well as a midwife wherever she went.

"I'm sure there's a lot you don't know about me," Bree said, then squeezed her lips together as if she wanted to take back the words.

"A woman of mystery. Well, you give me time and I bet I'll learn all those secrets you're keeping," Lucretia said. "Now, let me take you back to the exam offices so I can show you how I set up the supplies. Mind you, don't be wasting them. They don't grow on trees and the budget's tight for this place."

Knowing that Bree was in good hands, he left them to it and went back to top off his cup of coffee. The two women had just met, but already Bree was talking with Lucretia like the two of them were old friends. It seemed she was only prickly with him. So what was it about him that made the woman's back go up every time he was around? Was it because of who his parents were? He'd met a lot of people who were intimidated by his parents' fame, but he still didn't think she was one of them.

The door to their offices opened and he heard Lucretia welcome their first patient of the day. It looked like the mystery of Midwife Bree Rogers would just have to wait.

By lunchtime, Bree understood immediately why Knox had referred to Lucretia as the boss. From the time the first patient came through the door until when they took a thirty-minute break to swallow down some takeout, the woman had kept the line of patients that filled the small rooms organized and constantly moving.

Lori had told her that she would be starting off working one-on-one with Knox, but by the time they'd seen the first ten patients, Knox had assigned her one of the exam rooms as her own and told her to let him know if she needed him. It had felt good that he had confidence in her skills, even if she shouldn't have cared what he thought. Since then, she'd seen another six patients on her own and after figuring out the computer system for ordering lab tests and pharmacy prescriptions, she'd not had any trouble. She'd discovered quickly that most of the women the clinic saw were young and seeking an inexpensive way to obtain birth control or to be tested for STDs or pregnancy, all things that she'd been well trained in at the Legacy Clinic, though she'd quickly learned that giving these women a prescription didn't always mean the women could afford it.

When one woman she saw explained that the reason she had returned after being seen the month before was that she couldn't afford to get the birth control prescription filled, Bree had gone into the storage closet and taken out a six-month supply for the woman, along with a handful of condoms that she stuffed into the bag before the woman had left. The look on Lucretia's face when the woman walked out told Bree that the boss knew exactly what she had done and would be watching her. Giving the *boss* a guilty wave, Bree had slinked back into her assigned exam room to see her next patient. Yes, she knew they were working on a limited supply of samples of medication, but how much more wasteful would it be if the woman had to return every month? It would still be the same amount of samples given.

By the time they had stopped for their break, she was prepared to support her argument in case she was called on the carpet by either Lucretia or Knox.

"So, any issues?" Knox asked her as he handed her a canned drink and sandwich.

"No, it's all been good," she said, looking over at Lucretia. When the woman didn't say anything to the contrary, Bree figured she'd been worrying for nothing.

"I know this work isn't as exciting as delivering babies, but some of the women who come here have no place else to turn for basic care. My friend Dean, who runs this place, spends almost as much time working to get financing for supplies as he does seeing patients. I don't know exactly what his salary is, but if it's anything like what I receive when I'm working out in the small rural areas, it isn't much."

She'd only been working there a few hours, but already she could see that there was a true need in the community. How could one clinic that was only open two days a week provide for the needs of a city the size of Nashville?

"If you like the work, I know he would be happy to have the extra help," Knox said.

"I don't know what I'm going to do when I finish my residency. I have to pass my boards and then..." Had she really been about to say she had a little girl to take care of? "I just have a lot on my plate."

"I understand," Knox said, shrugging, before looking away. Bree had a strange feeling that she had disappointed him somehow.

"I'm sorry. I just can't commit to anything right now. I've been going nonstop for several years now and… I have other responsibilities that I need to take care of."

"It's okay, Bree. I didn't mean to put you on the spot. I just noticed that you seemed to be enjoying the job, and the patients seemed to be comfortable with you. But then I hear you've always been great with the patients at the clinic. You know I've helped start clinics like this one in the rural mountain towns where I've worked. I've even left some of them with a midwife in charge."

"Really?" she asked. "I'm surprised you could do that."

"The state of Tennessee allows midwives to work on their own without a doctor present. Of course, they all have doctors as resources and can refer out as needed. And not all the clinic services are free. If a patient has insurance, the clinic can file for reimbursement. A lot of their patients do have funding, they just don't have anywhere to go without traveling more than an hour."

"That sounds like an interesting job," Bree said. She could imagine herself living in a rural area someday. A place where Ally would have plenty of room to run and play.

"If you ever decide you're interested, get in contact with me. After watching you today, I think you might enjoy the work," Knox said.

Bree could feel the blush creep up her face with the compliment. Why did this man have to keep being so nice to her? She didn't want him to be nice. She wanted him to be…well, she didn't know what she wanted him to be, but she didn't want him to be like this. His being nice just increased the guilt and fear she had that everything she'd believed about him wasn't true. And that wasn't something she could consider.

Because if you've been wrong all this time, if this man would have been a proper parent for Ally, how are you going to live with the fact that you didn't contact him after Brittany's death? And what do you do about Ally then? Can you live with the guilt that you knew he was Ally's father and never told him? Or her?

It had been easy to keep silent about Ally when her father had been some undeserving sperm donor. But now, actually getting to know the man herself, she couldn't conceive that the man her sister had made sound so cold and uncaring was the same man sitting across from her. The same man who went across the country starting clinics for underserved communities.

And it wasn't just that she had taken Brittany's word. Bree had done some investigating herself. There was no doubt that Knox had gotten into trouble during his teenage years. It had been small things, but she knew those things usually grew to bigger things when a teenager got older. There were also reports of him going to rehab more than once. Had he really changed his life that much? From everything she had seen since meeting him, it seemed that he had.

Bree's hands began to shake as she lifted the sandwich toward her mouth. Her stomach protested at the thought of taking another bite. What was she going to do? Tell him about Ally? She'd promised her sister that she would keep her secret. How could she ignore her sister's last request?

"Are you okay?" Knox's hand reached out across the table, just stopping before it covered hers. "You look a little pale."

Looking up, her eyes met his and she bit

back a groan when she saw the concern there. "I'm fine. I'm just tired."

Her eyes remained locked on his and the guilt she'd felt earlier changed to something more disturbing. As she realized how close the two of them were, her unsteady stomach suddenly seemed to be filled with happy little butterflies performing an unfamiliar dance. Looking down, she saw his hand, strong and steady, so close to her own. She was shocked to find that she wanted to reach out her own hand and cover his. She wanted to feel that connection of skin to skin. She wanted to feel the warmth of his fingers slipping over hers. She wanted to find some comfort from this mess she'd made and the consequences she had to face.

"I hate to hear that," Lucretia said from the doorway, causing the both of them to jump, "because I've got a pregnant woman that just walked in saying she's having contractions, and I don't know nothing about delivering babies."

The two of them jumped up, with Knox beating her to the front of the office where a woman who looked not far from a full-term pregnancy was bent over at the waist.

"I tried to get her to sit down, but she won't budge," Lucretia said.

Even with her limited experience, Bree could see the woman was deep into laboring. She and Knox looked at each other. Gone was the intimacy she'd felt before. They were back to business. Thank goodness.

"Lucretia, call 911 and tell them we have a woman in labor," Knox said.

"What's your name?" Bree asked, putting her arm under the woman's to help support her when her pregnant body relaxed in relief as the contraction ended.

"Elena," the woman said, her dark brown eyes looking up at Bree. "My name is Elena. The pain, it's so hard."

"It's okay. There's an ambulance coming that will take you to the hospital where they can help with that. How many weeks are you?" Knox asked as he looped his arm around the woman's other side.

"The baby…he is due next month," the woman gasped out as another contraction started.

Half lifting, half dragging, they helped the woman into the first exam room, pausing when another contraction hit, causing her to double over with the pain.

Bree squatted down in front of her and took her hands. "Breathe with me. It will help."

Eyes drowning with the pain met Bree's, searching for help. "Let's get you up on the exam table so Dr. Collins can check to see how dilated you are."

Knox lifted the woman up while she gripped Bree's hand with a strength that seemed inhuman.

"Next contraction, we'll breathe together." As the next contraction hit, Bree coached the woman into deep breathing through it, Bree's eyes demanding the woman's dark brown ones to focus on her, as Lucretia and Knox helped set up for examination. "That was great. You are doing so good. You said the baby was a boy?"

"A boy, yes. A son," Elena said.

"The contractions are less than two minutes apart. That ambulance better get here fast," she said to Knox before another contraction hit her patient.

"Look at me," she told Elena, trying to keep the woman's focus centered on breathing.

"I don't think it's going to matter how fast the ambulance goes," Knox said. "Lucretia, get me some blankets and the emergency box."

Knox's words and the worried look in his eyes told her that something was wrong. As he mouthed the word *feet*, Bree's heart rate spiked and her hand tightened on the young woman's. A footling breech delivery was difficult and dangerous in the best of settings. Here? Where they had no anesthesia, no NICU nurses, no option except to deliver vaginally? This was the worst possible situation.

Lucretia rushed into the room carrying a box labeled emergency delivery and a stack of white hospital blankets.

"Elena, your baby is coming, but he's coming out with his feet first. I'm going to need you to listen closely to Dr. Collins so we can get him out safely. Can you do that for me?"

Elena nodded her head, fear replacing the pain in her eyes. Bree wanted to watch Knox work, to see what was happening. There were so many things that could go wrong. A prolapsed cord. Entrapment. Elena's baby was in real danger, but Bree knew she couldn't let her worry show. It was too important that Elena stayed in control. It could determine the baby's survival.

"Okay, Elena, you're going to feel a lot of pressure. I need to maneuver the baby the rest of the way out, but I don't want you to push. Just pay attention to Bree. She'll help you."

Bree's hands tightened on Elena's while placing her face inches from the other woman's. "You've got this, Elena."

"But the pressure..." Elena's voice broke on a groan.

"Look at me. You are going to pant with me now," Bree said, using her momma voice that told Ally she had better be listening to her. Elena's eyes returned to her and the two of them began to pant, their sounds filling the room.

"Come on, little guy, help me out here," Knox said, before Elena gasped, then collapsed back on the exam table.

"He's out!" Lucretia shouted from the end of the exam table as the sound of a faint cry, followed by a very loud, pissed-off wail, filled the room.

"He's okay," Elena said. "He's really okay?"

"He's fine," Knox said, holding up the screaming baby. Bree noticed that the baby was on the small side, but his color was turning a beautiful, healthy pink with his crying.

Her eyes met Knox's and at that moment something passed between them as they shared the joy of a new life coming into the world; something unlike anything she had ever experienced. It was as if pieces of a puzzle slid into place, bonding them together right then and there. She didn't want to look away, knowing that she would lose this shared moment when she did.

Voices came from the office entrance. The ambulance had finally arrived.

Minutes later Elena, with her son held tightly in her arms, was loaded up on the stretcher for their trip to the hospital. As soon as they left the exam room, Knox sank to the floor, his back pressed up against the exam table. Unable to stop herself, Bree followed him down.

"I was so afraid you wouldn't be able to get him out in time," she said.

"Me, too," Knox admitted, removing the gloves he still wore and dropping them on the floor. The room was a mess, but cleaning it could wait.

"I couldn't tell. You seemed so calm."

"We were lucky that the baby was small and it wasn't her first. The fact that we didn't have a prolapsed cord was a miracle. I don't know what I would have done if you hadn't been there to keep Elena in control. You were great with her. We made a great team, didn't we?"

"We did," she said.

Bree liked the fact that he included her, making her feel as if her part in helping to get the little one out was just as important as his.

"I'm a likeable guy, if you give me a chance."

Bree was afraid he was right. Even though she didn't want to admit it.

Lucretia rushed back into the room and stopped, seeing the two of them on the floor together. "What do y'all think you're doing? If you think the two of you are just going to lie around for the rest of the day, you better start thinking again. We've got a hallway of women waiting for me to open the door. We ain't got no time for the two of you peacocking around because y'all delivered a baby."

Turning, the woman headed out the door, calling back, "You got two minutes, then I'm letting in the horde."

"You're a tough taskmaster, Lucretia," Knox called after her.

"And if you make me stay after five you'll be paying me overtime," the woman called back.

The two of them looked at each other and Bree realized just how close they sat together. Close enough for her to see that there were little flecks of brown scattered throughout his light gray eyes that seemed to match the light brown hair that curled around his face. Her breath caught. He was a beautiful-looking man. She looked away, hoping he hadn't noticed her staring at him.

"I guess we had better get back to work," Knox said, standing and then offering her a hand.

Bree looked at the hand he held out. Something had changed between the two of them over the past few minutes. Working together to deliver Elena's baby had torn more chunks out of the wall of bitterness she had constructed to keep Ally and her safe from him, creating even more confusion inside her. A part of her wanted to build back those walls, to hold on to the anger and bitterness that Brittany had passed on to her. She needed to ignore everything she was beginning to learn about him. The other part of her knew she had to discover the truth. Was he really the kind, caring man he appeared to be? Had he changed so much from the man Brittany had described to her? How was she supposed to discover the real Knox Collins? Maybe working with him was a good idea after all. Maybe it was time she gave him a chance to prove that he could be a good father to Ally.

Looking back at his hand, they both knew that if she took it she would be acknowledging that things had changed between the two of them. Somehow, she knew there would never be any going back after this.

Swallowing down the fear of where accepting the friendship he offered would take her and how that could affect her and her niece's lives, Bree reached for his hand.

CHAPTER THREE

KNOX HAD JUST gotten home when his phone rang. Some part of him, some crazy part he needed to ignore, had hoped that it was Bree calling. Instead, he saw that it was his mother making her daily check in with him. Why his mom felt the need to make sure he was taking care of himself now, he didn't know, though he couldn't deny that a part of him still craved his mother's attention. Still, he'd tried to explain to her that he was a grown man who didn't need his mommy checking on him every day. She'd pushed back, telling him that if he had a wife she wouldn't feel the need to call every day. He'd dropped the argument, knowing he'd been outmaneuvered. His mother was an expert at that. They both knew that there had been a time when his parents had been so busy with their country music careers, that they hadn't given him the time or the supervision he'd needed. It wasn't a coincidence that the daily calls had started after his best friend had died from a car accident that he could easily have been in. Thad's death had affected all of them.

"Hi, Mom," he said as he opened the door to the fridge.

"Hello, darling, how was your day at the clinic?" His mother's voice warmed that part of him that went cold with memories of his friend.

"Interesting and very unexpected," he answered. "We delivered a baby on our lunch break."

"A baby? At the clinic? I thought this was a community clinic, not an OB clinic."

"Well, today we changed the rules." Knox stared inside the fridge. What was it he had been looking for?

"We? You mean the manager you told me about helped? I hope she wasn't traumatized. That's not what she signed up for, I'm sure."

"It was unexpected for all of us, but no. I meant the midwife who was working with me." Knox grabbed a bottle of water and shut the refrigerator door. "It was a difficult delivery. I don't know what I would have done if Bree hadn't been there to help keep the mother in control."

"You didn't tell me you had more staff. Tell

me more about this Bree. Is she married?" The hopefulness in his mother's voice set off all his warning bells.

"No. At least I don't think so." Bree didn't really talk much about anything outside of work, at least not around him. But there hadn't been a ring on her finger. He knew because he'd checked not long after they had met. Not that it had done any good. It had only taken a couple of weeks at the Legacy Clinic for him to realize the woman did not care for him at all. And that was putting it mildly. She'd shut him down the first conversation he'd tried to start with her, and things had only gone down from there.

"What's wrong? Is it this Bree woman?" his mother asked. He wondered sometimes why scientists hadn't been able to discover just where a mother's intuition was located. He had no doubt that it did exist.

"I don't understand her at all," Knox said before realizing the giant hole he'd left open for his mother's inquisition.

"Imagine, a man that doesn't understand a woman. I take it this isn't a work thing. You said she helped you with the delivery?"

Knox thought about the way she'd eyed his hand before she'd reached out to him. It had been just a friendly gesture, one that he would have offered to anyone. But with Bree, the way she'd studied it, it had felt like more. And then there'd been the feel of her hand in his. There'd been nothing friendly about the way his heart rate had spiked from the touch of her soft hand sliding inside his. If he'd held on for just a second too long, he didn't think she had noticed.

"No, not exactly work, it's just…" Knox didn't know how to describe the way Bree had reacted to him from day one. "She acts like I've done something to make her mad at me. Or as if somehow I've let her down. But it doesn't make sense. I'd never met her before I started working at Legacy."

"Are you sure of that?" his mother asked. "Women tend to remember more when it comes to, let's say, romantic interludes."

There had been a time when he'd been wild and reckless, and there were a lot of women who had come and gone in those days. But none of them had been Bree. He was sure of that. He'd remember her. Besides, Bree wasn't the kind of woman who ran after the town's bad boy that he'd been then. She was smarter than that.

"I'm sure. Don't worry about it. It could all be my imagination," Knox said, though he knew it wasn't. "Tell me about Dad. Is he still obsessed with his new golf clubs?"

As his mother talked about his father's golf swing, as well as the new putting green he was insisting they have put in, Knox found himself thinking again about the way Bree had sat so still as she'd studied the hand he'd held out to her, as if she feared taking his offer of help. But it had been more and he'd known it. He'd been extending a hand in friendship.

And even though she'd taken his hand and he knew something had changed between the two of them after working together in the clinic, he couldn't help but think whatever it was she was holding against him was going to come out eventually.

Bree turned around as her name was called from across the bar. Waving to a customer she'd been dodging for the past fifteen minutes, she shouted over the noisy crowd, "I'll be right there."

Was the place exceptionally loud tonight, or was it just that she was getting too old for the job? There was a time, when she was young and just beginning college, that working at The Dusty Jug in downtown Nashville on a Friday night had been the perfect job. Now, after ten years of slinging beers and dealing with the occasionally rowdy tourist, she could do the job on autopilot, something that she found herself doing more and more lately. Being a single mom, a midwife resident and fill-in bar staff was getting to be too much for her. The lack of sleep was beginning to wear on her.

But what were her options? She had food, rent and childcare to pay for and the tips at the bar were good on weekends. If she could just hold on for a few more months, she'd be able to have a normal schedule. Well, as normal as a midwife's schedule could be.

"Is that guy bothering you?" Mack asked from behind the bar.

"He's just another guy who's partied a little too much this weekend. I can handle him." Bree had been handling men like him for years now. The best way to deal with him was to serve him his beer with a smile, then walk away as fast as she could. The place was so busy tonight that she wouldn't have to worry about him following her through the crowd.

Bree delivered an order, then went over to the table where the man who'd waved her down sat with three of his friends, all of them in different states of inebriation. She'd bet her tip money on the three of them being college students who were celebrating the end of the semester. They'd all regret it in the morning, but there wouldn't be any convincing them of that tonight. "What can I get you?"

"How about your number?" the young man asked, then elbowed his friend when he started to laugh.

"Sorry, not tonight," she said. "But I will give you the number to a car service as there is no way any of you are driving home tonight."

"I've got one," one of the other men stated, waving his phone up in the air toward her.

"Okay, then," she said, turning to leave, only to have the one closest to her grab her arm.

"One more round?" he asked, giving her a smile that made him look even younger.

She looked down at his hand pointedly, and he immediately let go.

"Sorry, ma'am," he said, his eyes dropping from hers.

"One more, then you call for a ride," she said, then pointed over to Danny, the bouncer on duty. "I'm telling him to keep an eye on y'all and make sure you get a safe ride home. No more bars, either. You all go home."

All four heads turned toward the man standing at the door. Six feet five and over two hundred fifty pounds, Danny had played offense for the Vanderbilt Commodores back in his college days and now coached football at one of the local high schools. He was all muscle, and wearing a skintight T-shirt, he proved he was not afraid to show it off. Anyone who thought they'd act out at the Dusty Jug changed their mind when Danny looked their way.

Heading back to the bar for their order, she was stopped when Sara, one of the other waitresses, flagged her down. "Mack said the band is running fifteen minutes late and he wants you to cover for them."

"That's the third time this month. Mack needs to do something about them." It wasn't that Bree minded entertaining the crowd. She'd been doing it for years and Mack would make sure the band gave her a share of their tips. And even when the bar was busy like tonight, it wasn't the same as getting up on a concert stage where those huge blinding lights kept you from seeing the people you were supposed to be performing for. "Can you take care of the group at table twenty? Tell Mack they only get one more round, he knows what they're drinking, and then they're out of here."

"Got it," Sara said, rushing back to the bar.

After stopping to give Danny a heads-up on the group of young men in case they tried to sneak past the bouncer, she headed back to the staff lounge where she kept her guitar stashed for times like this. She stopped by a mirror and couldn't help but remember that first time she'd gone on stage, dressed up in that ridiculous pink dress, with her sister beside her. Life hadn't turned out the way any of them had expected then. Her dreams and her sister's had been so different. Her sister loved the stage from the moment they'd walked out in front of those glaring spotlights, while Bree had only wanted to run off stage and hide in their dressing room until it was all over.

She couldn't help but ask herself if things would have been different for Brittany if Bree had just gone along with her sister's plans. Yes, Bree wouldn't have been happy with a life in the spotlight. But would that have been so bad if it meant she would still have her sister?

Thinking about Brittany as she climbed up on the small platform that acted as the bar's stage, Bree ran her fingers over the guitar strings, making adjustments before picking out a song she'd written one night after her sister had died. She'd never sung it in public, it wasn't a bar kind of song, but when her fingers played the intro to the song she had written so long ago, she began to sing.

* * *

Knox hadn't been crazy about a night of bar hopping. He'd left that scene years ago and had never looked back. But it was his cousin's bachelor party; his attendance had been demanded. Now, after two hours of going from one overcrowded bar to another, he was already planning his escape. He'd spent too much of the first years of his college life at bars, something he was still trying to live down. With his reputation as a doctor always on the line, he was now aware of everything he did. He never wanted to be thought of as Nashville's rebellious bad boy again.

As he followed his cousin and his friends into the next bar on their list, he felt a change in the atmosphere. The Dusty Jug was packed, but instead of the normal rowdy crowd of the other bars, the place was almost silent except for the voice of a young woman singing. Unable to see the stage from where he stood at the entrance, he weaved his way through the crowd, drawn by a voice so sweet and pure, yet for some reason familiar.

Finding a place against the bar, he craned his neck to the side to see a young woman with a guitar in her arms, playing a song whose words spoke of a deep pain of loss. Just the sound of her voice made you want to weep.

"You left me with an angel to heal my heart." The woman sang the chorus, then started on another verse. "When you got your wings, you left an angel with your eyes, your laugh. You left an angel so that I'd always have you with me. As long as your little angel is with me, I'll always have an angel to heal my heart."

As the woman played the last notes then looked up at the crowd, Knox's breath seized in his lungs, his heart stuttering from shock. The crowd's enthusiastic cheers jerked him back to reality and he sucked in a breath. Sitting on the stage, Bree Rogers smiled and thanked everyone before standing as a group of musicians began to take the stage.

Her hair was pulled back into a ponytail, the same way she wore it at work. But with her white T-shirt, cutoff jean shorts and white tennis shoes, she looked too young to even be allowed in the bar, let alone old enough to be delivering babies.

Then he remembered the pain he'd seen in her eyes as she sang. A pain he knew spoke of a heartache she was definitely too young to have experienced. He recognized that pain. It was the pain of loss. He had carried the weight of that pain since the unnecessary death of his best friend. It had been almost nine years and it hadn't gotten any easier.

He watched as she moved toward the bar, then stopped when she spotted him. For a few seconds neither of them moved. None of this made sense. What was the midwife doing here entertaining a bar crowd? He'd never heard anything about her being able to sing like that, either. Not that there weren't thousands of people who had come to Nashville to get a break into the country music world. But he couldn't believe Bree was one of them. Just the little bit he'd worked with her proved that her dedication was to midwifery.

"What are you doing here?" she asked, suspicion in her eyes. Did she think he was stalking her?

"Bachelor party," he said. "What about you?"

She looked down at the T-shirt she wore that displayed the bar's name. "It should be pretty obvious that I work here."

She moved past him and said something to the bartender before turning back to him. "I've got to get back to work. Enjoy your party."

He watched as she walked off, her head held high as she balanced a tray of drinks. He spotted his group at the back of the bar where they'd managed to find a table and went to join them. The mystery of Brianna Rogers just kept getting bigger and bigger. He knew he should let it go. Bree deserved her privacy. But he couldn't seem to do it. The more he learned about her, the more he wanted to know.

It wasn't that hard to figure out that she had to be working at the bar to pay the bills. He didn't know anything about her past. He'd had rich parents to support him while he was in school; most students didn't. But the music, the voice, that was the surprise. Instead of waiting tables, she could have been singing anywhere in Nashville with that voice.

"I saw you talking to that waitress. You know her?" his cousin said, leaning over toward Knox while the other men were busy with a conversation about their golf game that day.

"I thought I did, but now I'm not so sure." But he would. Somehow, someway, he would find out everything there was to know about Brianna. Then maybe this obsession with her would end.

He studied the drink in front of him, refusing to let her catch him studying her. He didn't want her to think he really was stalking her. She might not have accused him of it, but the look she'd given him had spoken of a mistrust.

Was it possible that she had a history of being stalked? That would explain a lot about her behavior, not only here, but also at the office. Maybe a bad experience had her keeping her distance from all men.

"I don't know what the two of you have going on, but some guy over there seems to be giving her a hard time," his cousin said, starting to stand.

Knox looked up and saw a young man slam his empty drink glass down on the table then stand. Knox put a hand on his cousin's shoulder and pushed him back into the chair before standing. "Your momma will kick my butt if you get in a bar fight and mess up your pretty face tonight. I've got this."

Most of the crowd was settled around the stage where the band played, making it easy for Knox to cross the room to where Bree was arguing with a kid who had plainly drunk more than he should. He looked over to where the bouncer on duty was busy dealing with three other guys about the same age. They all looked like they were about to fall over. Knox could still remember those days of being old enough to drink legally, but not smart enough to know when to stop.

"Is there a problem?" he asked as he approached. With Bree's hands on her hips and her eyes shooting fire, Knox was glad he wasn't the one in her sights.

Without looking at him, Bree waved him away. "Cooper doesn't want to leave with his friends. For some reason, he thinks I have to serve him a drink even though I've already told him he was cut off."

Knox took in the relaxed way she stood. She wasn't really intimidated by this guy. She was just looking out for the kid and he was too drunk to see it. "Well, Cooper, it sounds like it's time to thank your waitress for her service, leave a big tip for her trouble and head home before you do something that you'll regret in the morning."

When the boy turned, swinging wildly, Knox's arms came up instinctively while he moved himself in front of Bree. The boy's swing met air and the rest of his body followed through, sending him sprawling on to the bar floor.

The sound of Bree's whistle carried over the band and both the bartender and the bouncer headed their way. Within minutes, the kid was off the floor and headed outside with the bouncer, who had assured Knox that the kid and his friends would be tucked into a car from a local service.

"Are you okay?" he asked Bree, once the bar doors closed behind the bouncer.

"I'm fine. I've seen worse," Bree said, then glanced up from where she was gathering empty glasses from the table. "How about you?"

"Unfortunately, I've seen worse, too.' He tried to keep his voice calm, but he couldn't help but think about the night he and Thad had been out drinking in a bar not much different than this one. Who knows, they might have come to this bar that night. They'd both been too young and dumb to know when they'd reached their limit then. Maybe if someone like Bree had stopped Thad from stumbling outside and getting into his car, his friend would still be here. It had only been the fact that Knox had run into a group from his parents' band that had saved him from joining his friend.

"You sure you're okay?" Bree asked. She'd moved in front of him, dipping her head down until her eyes met his. There was worry in her eyes now. Worry for him.

"Sorry, just memories from long ago when me and my friends thought we knew everything, too," he said. She moved back from him and picked up her tray that she'd loaded with glasses. She started to walk away, back toward the bar, and he tried to find a reason to stop her. "Thank you for looking out for that kid. I wish there'd been someone like you that night."

Turning, she gave him a quizzical look. "What night?"

They stood there, standing in the middle of a bar, and for some reason Knox couldn't stop himself from spilling his guts. "Me and my friend went out partying one night, though we should have been back at the dorm studying for exams. Thad said we'd cram the next day. I was young and stupid. I had dreams of medical school, but I was messing them up. I agreed with him. There was plenty of time for studying. I didn't even try to talk him out of going out. I'd spent most of that year partying instead of studying. I still don't know how I graduated that year."

"What happened?" she asked.

Knox looked around, before looking up at Bree. "You had to have heard all the reports of the wild son of Charles and Gail Collins."

From high school to the day Thad had died, he'd given his parents nothing but trouble. All in the name of a "good time." Back then, if there was a bar fight in downtown Nashville, he had probably been in it. That had been what he thought was a good time.

He didn't want to think about those times. He didn't want to remember that last night when Thad had thrown his arm over Knox's shoulder and told him he'd see him the next day. He didn't want to think about letting his friend walk out, knowing that his friend was as drunk as he was, and never making a move to stop him.

"I let my best friend, as drunk as those kids who just left, walk out of the bar, knowing that he was going to drive himself home. He never made it there."

He saw the shock in her eyes, then the pity that followed. He didn't need her pity. Didn't deserve it.

"Anyway, thanks for watching out for guys like Cooper. I hope someday he realizes he owes you a thank-you." Knox turned and walked back to the table where he could see his cousin's friends were finishing their drinks and getting ready to move on.

He felt raw from the memories and irritated at himself for letting his guard down in front of Bree. He was Dr. Collins now. Her mentor. She needed to trust his guidance. He didn't need to dig up all his past sins for her to see.

He'd fought too hard to turn his life around. His memories were of a past he had tried to bury. So why did it feel so important that he share them with Bree?

CHAPTER FOUR

WHEN BREE WOKE up Tuesday morning, she was surprised to find that she was looking forward to a day at the community clinic. Not that she didn't still have reservations about working with Knox; after their conversation at the bar she was more confused than ever. No matter how much she wanted to ignore it, the Knox Collins she was getting to know was not the same one that her sister had known.

But how could someone change that much? Oh, she could understand that Knox had changed his ways as far as being totally centered on partying while he was in college. A lot of kids went down that road before waking up and discovering life wasn't all partying. Bree had no doubt that her sister had been right there in the partying crowd. It was probably where Brittany had met Knox. But there was something else that bothered her. Bree knew Brittany's thirst for fame had always been her sister's driving force. She'd always wondered if Brittany had really just run across Knox at a bar one night, or had she sought him out knowing that Knox's parents could help her in her drive for her career? It was a terrible thing to think about her sister, but Bree had personally seen the things Brittany would do for her career. She had to be honest with herself.

But did it really matter what Brittany's reasons were? Her sister was gone. It was only Ally who mattered now. Her niece would someday look at her and ask about her daddy. And what was Bree to say then? That she'd promised Ally's mother that she'd never tell her father about her? Was it really fair to the child for Bree to hold back information that would affect her whole life? Was it fair to Knox? She knew the answer to both questions. She knew she had to do the right thing for both Ally and Knox. She just didn't know if she had the courage to do it.

Bree was still struggling with her thoughts when she walked into the clinic and was greeted by Lucretia.

"Well, what are you doing coming in here looking like your best friend just died?" Lucretia asked when Bree entered the office with none of the excitement she'd felt that morning.

Instead, she felt the weight of years of keeping a secret that she never should have been forced to keep.

"What's wrong?" Lucretia asked, all her teasing gone now.

Bree's mouth refused to move as her throat tightened and her eyes began to water. She looked around the room, beginning to panic. The last thing she needed was for Knox to find her having a meltdown in the waiting room.

"Come on," Lucretia said, then gestured for Bree to follow her back into one of the exam rooms.

"Sit. You've got five minutes to tell me what's wrong. I can't have you bringing problems here that might affect your work," the woman said as she pointed to an old plastic chair against the back wall. While the woman's words could have seemed cold, her eyes were full of concern.

Bree looked at the chair then back at Lucretia, who stood against the door and Bree's only escape. At that moment Bree realized why she'd come to like the woman so much. Lucretia's take-charge attitude reminded her of her momma's. But while her momma had become blinded by the glitz of the country music world and her dreams for Bree's and Brittany's music career, Lucretia was only looking out for her and the patients at the clinic.

"It's nothing. I'm here to work. I just have some things on my mind." Even as she spoke the words, she wished she could say more. She'd kept her sister's secret for so long. And for what? Everything her sister said wasn't true now, which left Bree with a terrible burden that she didn't think she could carry any longer. "I've done something, something that I thought was the right thing at the time. I kept a secret that I shouldn't have. Now I think I was wrong. Now I have some hard decisions to make because what I've done has affected other people's lives."

Bree swallowed, then forced herself to continue. "And the truth is I'm afraid."

There. She'd said the two words she'd refused to admit even to herself. She was afraid. Afraid of breaking a sacred promise she'd made to her sister just days before Brittany had been killed. Afraid of confronting Knox with the news that he had a daughter. Afraid of telling Ally that she'd had a father her whole life who didn't know about her. But most of all, she was afraid of losing a child that was as much hers as she was Brittany's and Knox's. Whether it had been the right thing to do or not, Bree had raised Ally as her child. And the thought of losing her scared her most of all.

Looking up, Bree saw Lucretia's eyes soften. "Girl, being afraid is part of living. And sometimes it's part of doing the right thing. We don't know each other that well, but I don't think you would have done something to hurt someone. At least, not on purpose."

Bree shook her head. "Just because it wasn't on purpose doesn't mean it won't hurt them."

"Which will hurt them more? Admitting to them that you made a mistake? Or continuing to keep a secret they have the right to know?"

Bree knew the answer to Lucretia's question. She'd already made the decision that she had to tell both Ally and Knox the secret she'd promised never to tell. She had to do the right thing by both of them. Now she just had to figure out how.

"Lucretia? Bree?" Knox's voice called from down the hall. "Where is everybody?"

Bree knew that there was no way that Lucretia could know that her secret involved Knox, but the sound of his voice sent warning signals to her brain while at the same time she felt the heavy weight of guilt in her chest. "Please don't mention any of this to him."

"Anything I hear in these office walls is privileged information, isn't it?" Lucretia asked, then winked at her before the exam door opened and Knox stuck his head inside.

"Is there an office meeting I wasn't notified of?" Knox asked, his voice light and teasing.

"No," Bree said, rushing past the two of them to escape. In a matter of minutes, Lucretia had helped her narrow down the answer to her problem to the simplest of answers. She had to do the right thing, no matter how scared she was.

But first, she had to come up with a plan. It wasn't every day that a man learned he had an eight-year-old daughter. Would he be happy? Angry? He'd certainly be angry that Brittany, and then Bree, hadn't told him about the pregnancy, because the more she got to know Knox, the more she was convinced that he had never known about Brittany's pregnancy. She could understand that he'd be angry with her and she deserved his anger. But no matter how angry he was, they would still have to work together. And they'd have to figure out a way to tell Ally.

They'd have to do that together, too, she decided as she went into the second exam room, pretending to organize the supplies, though she had no doubt Lucretia had seen to that earlier.

Finally, the first patient arrived and her busy

day began. Putting her personal problems aside, she focused all of her energy on her patients. Avoiding Knox wasn't a problem. The two of them were kept too busy to even stop for a break.

After seeing twice the number of patients that she saw in a day at the Legacy Clinic, she'd thought her day over when Lucretia found her in one of the exam rooms setting up for their next clinic day. "There's a girl, she can't be eighteen, that has been pacing outside the office for the last thirty minutes. I tried to talk to her, but she ran off. Now she's back. Can you talk to her and see what she needs?"

Looking at her watch, Bree saw that she was due to pick up Ally in less than an hour. She couldn't be late getting there, again. It seemed she never had enough time anymore.

Both she and Knox were scheduled at the Legacy Clinic the next day, as Lori had rearranged Bree's office and call schedule around Knox's so that Bree could continue to work with her two days a week. And while Bree was happy that she was getting the experience she needed, it was getting harder and harder for her to manage her work at the two clinics, her job at the Dusty Jug and make sure Ally was given the attention she needed.

"She looks scared, Bree. And she's very skittish. I don't want to scare her away again." Bree had only known the office manager for a couple days, but she had already learned to trust Lucretia's instincts.

"I'll try to talk to her. Maybe I can get her to come back next week when we are open." Bree said, before heading to the small office waiting room where she could see the shadow of someone outside the frosted glass front door.

Not wanting to scare the girl, Bree opened the door slowly then stepped out into the hall, shutting the door quietly behind her. The girl, looking closer to seventeen than eighteen if you ignored the heavily made-up face, was thin. Too thin.

The girl's eyes met Bree's and Bree knew the girl was about to make a run for it. Stepping in front of her, Bree tried to stop her, holding out her hands to the girl. "Wait. I just want to help you."

But Bree could see that the girl wasn't listening. As the girl rushed past her, pushing Bree over as she passed, Bree caught a glimpse of big brown eyes that were filled with terror.

Bree had never seen anything like the look on the girl's face, and on instinct she had pushed away from the wall and started after the girl when the office door opened and Knox rushed out, Lucretia following right behind him.

"What's going on?" he asked, grabbing a hold of Bree's arm to steady her.

"I'm not sure," Bree said, though her mind was flooded with a hundred scenarios, none of them good. "There was a girl, a teenager, but she ran as soon as I tried to talk to her."

Bree looked up into his eyes. "She's in danger, Knox. I don't know what kind, but she's afraid of something. Or someone."

"Maybe she came to the clinic for birth control or because she thinks she's pregnant and she's afraid her parents will find out. Let me see if I can find her," Knox said, then let go of her arm and headed down the hall toward the stairs at a jog.

While Lucretia went back to shut down the office, Bree waited for Knox to return. When she saw him coming back down the hall, alone, her hopes that he had caught up with the girl died.

"She had too much of a head start for you to catch her," Bree said when he walked up. "I've dealt with the teenagers at Legacy House and others while I was working in the hospital as a nurse. I haven't ever had one react that way. Not with that amount of fear."

She had been more likely to get attitude from her teenage patients, at least at first. It usually took a while before you would figure out that it was mostly fear of what their bodies were going through or how their lives were about to change that was responsible for those attitudes. But she'd never seen such a hopeless fear on anyone's face as she'd seen on that young girl's.

"Maybe she'll be back Tuesday, when the clinic is open again," Knox said, though he looked as worried as Bree. "There's nothing we can do about it now."

The phone alarm on Bree's watch went off, reminding her that she had to leave then or she'd be late for after-school pickup. Silencing it, she saw that Knox was studying her.

"You're not working a shift at the bar tonight, are you?" he asked. "You have to be back at Legacy Clinic tomorrow."

Was she imagining the censorship in his voice? Was he suggesting that she shouldn't be working at the bar when she had to be at the clinic the next day? "I only work at the bar when I have the next day off, but that's really not any of your business, is it?"

"I'm sorry. You're right. I just think working

at the bar while you're doing your residency could be a problem. You need to be at your best, especially if you have a labor patient."

Bree chose to ignore the concern in his eyes. What right did this man have to judge her? She felt the anger at his words as it boiled out of her. She'd worked her butt off getting to where she was. She'd spent years juggling a child, school and a job. To suggest that she would do anything to jeopardize her career, or more importantly a patient, was insulting.

"You don't know anything about me, Knox." The heat in her face and the dangerous rate of her heart told her that she was about to go ballistic on the man. The anger drove her to take a step, then another. She was so close now that she would swear she could hear the beat of his heart. Or was that sound the beat of her own racing heart? Her breaths came faster as her eyes met his. Her hands came up to rest on his chest. They both stood there a minute while her anger warred with something else. Something more dangerous than her anger. For a second she couldn't remember where she was or why she was angry. All she knew was something changed in her, in him, when their eyes met. When his eyes dropped lower to rest on her lips, she felt herself sway toward him. Was he thinking about kissing her? She was surprised to find that she wanted him to. She wanted Knox to kiss her. It didn't make any sense, but she couldn't deny it. She was attracted to the last person she had these feelings for.

No. She couldn't do this. That was wrong. Nothing had changed between them. It was just something she had imagined. This was just a flood of hormones that had been brought on by her anger.

Her hands fell away from him. Her back stiffened. She forced her eyes away from him. She was too strong, too smart, to let a bunch of hormones take control of her like this.

Turning, she walked back into the clinic and grabbed her backpack, passing him where he still stood in the hallway. Refusing to look at him, she started toward the stairwell. She'd only gone a few feet before she heard him call after her.

"You're right. I don't know you, Bree," he called out behind her, "but I want to. I want to know everything about you."

Bree's feet faltered as her heart stuttered for a second. What did those words mean? And did she really want to know? She made her feet continue down the hall. While Knox might not know it, soon he would know more about her than he had ever dreamed possible. She just hoped that what was left between them when he did learn the truth about what she had done wasn't the nightmare she feared.

Knox knew that Bree was back to her old ways of avoiding him the next day. He'd hoped after the time they'd spent at the clinic, and after their talk at the bar, that things had changed between the two of them. Of course, it was probably his stupid confession that he wanted to get to know her better that had changed things. They'd just begun to get into a nice rhythm working together at the clinic, so why had he gone and ruined it? Maybe because it was the truth? Maybe because as they'd stood together in that hallway, with her hand pressed against his chest, all he could think about was wanting her to stay there, touching him. When she'd moved away from him, he'd felt the distance between them as acute as having a part of himself ripped away.

Bree Rogers not only fascinated him in a way no woman had ever done before, she also made him feel a longing he didn't know was possible. She was more pretty than beautiful, more sweet than sophisticated. In other words, nothing like the women he normally found himself attracted to. There was something special about her that he couldn't describe. And when she looked into his eyes it was as if she could see into his soul. He just wished he knew what it was she saw. Was it the boy he'd been who had never thought of others or of the consequences of what he did? Or was it the man he'd worked so hard to become? From the way she seemed to avoid him, he was afraid it was the former instead of the latter. Would he ever be able to put his past behind him?

"Do you have a moment, Knox?" Jack called out to him as Knox passed the senior Dr. Warner's office.

"Sure. I'm just headed over to the hospital to check on a postsurgical patient before I leave for the day. What's up?" Knox said, stepping into the older man's office.

"I know that you only have a few more weeks before your contract is up and Dr. Hennison returns. I just wanted to touch base with you and see what your plans were."

Knox took the seat in front of Jack's desk. "I've had some requests from some of the general practitioners up in the Smoky Mountains for me to return. I've been thinking of starting a type of travel practice where I can set up a home base in a central location, but still travel to some of the outlying areas where it's hard for people to get down to an office for a visit."

The two of them discussed the shortage of OB/GYN practices in the rural parts of the country for several minutes and what more the government could do to help encourage practitioners to move to those areas. Both of them agreed that a solution needed to be found for the women who didn't have access to the prenatal care they needed, due a lot to the cost of liability insurance.

"And what about Bree? How is she doing at the county clinic? I know she wasn't happy at first about the opportunity, but I thought the two of you would make a good team there. I hope you've been able to change her mind."

Knox was pretty sure that he'd destroyed the teamwork that they had been developing by admitting his interest in her, but he wasn't about to discuss that with Jack. And he knew she was mad at him over his questioning her about her need to work at the bar. He wasn't even sure if the practice was aware that Bree was working outside her commitment to them. But as he had been told, it wasn't his business. "She's doing well. The patients like her and she has a lot of empathy for their situation. Not everyone does."

"Well, that's good to hear. From everything I hear from Lori, she's going to make a good midwife," Jack said as his phone rang. Looking at the number, he shook his head. "It's my son. Always worrying I'm working too much."

"I have a mom for that. It's nice to know someone cares, isn't it?" Knox laughed, then stood and started out the door before Jack waved him to wait after telling his son to hold a moment.

"If you change your mind and decide to stay in town, let us know. We'd be happy to have you join the practice permanently," Jack said.

"It's a tempting offer, sir. Maybe one day I'll take you up on it. But for now, I think I'm needed in the mountains." He'd wondered if he'd get an offer from the practice and he hadn't been sure until that moment what he'd do if it came. Living close to his parents was tempting. His mother reminded him constantly that he wasn't getting any younger and needed to settle down. But just talking to Jack about the opportunity to make a difference in the rural communities of the mountains got him excited. That was where he was truly needed.

"I can't blame you for that. If I was twenty years younger, I think I'd join you. The mountains are beautiful this time of year and the work you're going to be doing will make a lot of difference for those communities," Jack said before returning to his call.

Knox stepped out the office door, only to find Bree standing in the middle of the hall.

"You're leaving?" she asked, her look intense and her tone demanding. "When?"

"I didn't know you cared," Knox teased, then stopped when he realized she was seriously upset. "I'm not leaving today. Jack just wanted to know my plans after I finish my contract here. What's wrong?"

Bree wasn't sure what was wrong. Knox's leaving was the answer to all her problems. If he wasn't there, the guilt she felt every time she looked at him would go away. Except, that wasn't true. She'd told herself that she was going to be honest with him. She was going to tell him about Ally. His leaving would complicate that in a lot of ways. The worst way being if he decided that he wanted to fight for custody of Ally and wanted to take her away with him, something that she hadn't considered until now. Her stomach protested at the thought, her insides doing a somersault. She couldn't face the possibility of Ally being taken from her.

But she couldn't explain any of this to Knox.

Not yet. "I just need to know if I'll be working with you at the clinic for the next three weeks like we had planned."

"Like I said, I'm not leaving till my contract is over."

"Good," she said. She sounded like someone with only two functioning brain cells. "I mean, it's good that you'll be there to work in the clinic."

"Are you okay?" Knox asked, his eyes studying her too closely. "You look tired."

"Well, thank you for that. That's just what every woman wants to hear." After another night of tossing and turning, she hadn't been surprised to find the dark shadows under her eyes. She'd told herself that she wasn't sleeping because of her decision to tell Knox about Ally, but she'd awakened more than once from dreams about Knox that had her pushing the covers off her overheated body. She couldn't forget the way she'd felt when Knox had brushed his finger down her cheek. The way her body had responded when he'd just looked at her lips. If he'd kissed her at that moment, she would have gone up in flames.

"I'm just concerned about you. You're doing a lot between the clinic and working at the bar," said Knox, his eyes lingering on those shadows.

The concern in his voice just made her feel worse about her deception. Guilt was eating her up inside. She had to move forward with her plan to tell Knox about Ally. She had to ignore all other feelings she had for Knox and concentrate on the fact that he was her niece's father.

And the first thing she had to do was to introduce him to Ally. "Are you going to be at the cleanup day at Legacy House this weekend?"

"I'm planning on it," Knox said. "I think everyone that isn't on call is coming. It seems to be a big office project."

"That's good. It sounds like they'll need all the volunteers they can get," she said, then began walking backward, away from him. "I guess I'll see you there, then."

"Okay, it's a date," he said, giving her a smile that sent her libido into overdrive. Then the evil man winked at her before walking away, leaving Bree in shock as she stood and watched him go.

What had just happened? Was the man flirting with her now? He wasn't serious. He'd just been joking. Hadn't he? He didn't really think she'd been trying to get a date with him.

Slowly, she walked away, her mind filled with scenes of Knox Collins and his dangerously wicked smile.

CHAPTER FIVE

BREE HELPED ALLY pull the wagon they'd filled with small tree limbs the two of them had picked up from the backyard of Legacy House. She had told Ally that she wanted to introduce her to the doctor she worked with at the clinic, hoping to somehow smooth Knox and the little girl's introduction before she revealed to the two of them that they were father and daughter. Now the little girl asked every few minutes if "that doctor" was there yet. Bree was starting to think that she had been stood up, which was crazy. It wasn't a real date. Knox had just been teasing her. Still, she caught herself looking up from their work every time a new car drove into the driveway of the home.

They'd been working for almost an hour, when a dark blue truck stopped in front of the house and parked. Her breath caught when a jean-clad Knox climbed out. Dolly Parton's song about a man with a cowboy hat and painted-on jeans showing up to tempt her started playing in Bree's mind. Knox was every bit tempting as any man she had ever seen. He'd pulled his hair back into a tiny tail at the back of his head, giving him the look of a young rogue in one of her historical romances.

"Aunt Bree, who's that guy? Is he your doctor?" Ally asked from beside her.

That question got her full attention. If someone had told her six months ago that she would be standing there, about to introduce Ally to the man who was her father, Bree would never have believed it. Knox's finding out about the little girl was a nightmare that she would have run from. But now, after getting to know him, she knew she was doing the right thing.

Not that she was going to tell either of them about their relationship yet. She had to go about that more cautiously. First, she wanted them to meet. She wanted Knox to see that Ally was a happy girl and that Bree was taking good care of her. Then she would tell him. After that, she'd see where they went. She thought that it would be best if Bree and Knox told Ally together, but that would all depend on how things went with Knox first. There was a probability that Knox would want to get a DNA test before he accepted that Ally was his. And while

Bree had no doubt that Brittany had told the truth about Ally being his child, she couldn't blame him for wanting proof.

"He's not my doctor. He's the doctor I work with at the clinic downtown. The one I told you about. Do you want to meet him now?" Bree asked the little girl, who was studying Knox as he greeted one of the other volunteers. She watched as he opened the bed of his truck and began to remove bags of soil, throwing two of them over his shoulder before he headed their way.

"Sure," Ally said, then headed off to where some of the other children were helping to pull the weeds out of a flower garden that ran the length of the front porch. It seemed Ally wasn't as impressed as Bree was by Knox's arrival.

She knew the moment he saw her, their eyes meeting and his lighting up as he gave her a grin before handing the bags of soil over to the man next to him and then returning back to the truck where he opened the back door. She watched as he reached into the backseat and came out with a small pot containing a beautiful royal blue orchid. Turning, he looked back at her, smiling as he headed toward her.

"I'm not usually late for my dates," he said,

holding out the ceramic pot with the beautiful flower. "This is for you."

Bree looked at the potted plant, then back up at his smiling face. Had the man been serious when he'd called their meeting together today a date? Or was he still teasing her?

Guilt flooded through her system, as a nasty knot formed in her chest. What was she doing? She'd thought that getting to know Knox would be a good way to help her decide what to do about her niece, but the more she got to know him, the more she liked him. Now she thought of him as more than Ally's father, and more than just a work colleague. Now she was venturing into a place that could turn into a nightmare. The sooner she told Knox about Ally, the better for both of them. She just needed to give them time to get to know each other first. And she needed to build a relationship between her and Knox so that when she did approach him with the truth, he would be more open to listening to all the reasons she needed to remain as Ally's guardian.

Using that excuse, she reached out and took the plant, her hand brushing against Knox's, sending a tingle of awareness through her.

"What's that, Aunt Bree?" Ally asked from

beside her, startling her. "Are you going to plant it in the flower beds?"

"Not this one," Bree said. "It's an orchid. We have to keep it inside and take good care of it."

"Well, hello," Knox said. "What's your name?"

Bree's heart expanded with something she refused to name at the kindness in Knox's eyes as he bent down to the little girl's level. Ally and Knox's first meeting would forever be a bittersweet memory that she hoped she would never feel the need to regret.

"I'm Ally. Are you Aunt Bree's doctor?" Ally asked, her face studying Knox's with a seriousness beyond her years.

"I'm one of the doctors your aunt works with," Knox said.

"Okay," Ally said, before turning to her aunt. "Is he the doctor you wanted me to meet?"

Knox stood and looked up at Bree, one eyebrow lifting as his lips turned up in a teasing smile. "Am I the doctor you wanted her to meet?"

Bree chose to ignore his teasing. "This is Dr. Collins, and yes, he's the doctor I've told you about. The one I work with at the clinic where the women come in for help."

"You didn't say he was pretty," Ally said,

cutting her eyes to look over at Knox. "Don't you think he's pretty, Aunt Bree?"

Now the two of them were teasing her, surprising, since Bree had never known her niece to be teasing like this before. She was even more surprised to find that both Ally and Knox shared the same expression on their face. Both expectant. Both waiting to see what she was going to say next.

"Well, look at that," Bree said, adopting their playful manner, "I've never noticed before, Ally, but I think you might be right. He is kind of pretty."

Knox laughed and Ally giggled before running off to where one of the volunteers had started to help some of the kids spread the soil in the beds that they were preparing to plant flowers.

"I didn't know you had a niece," Knox said as they stood there together with Bree feeling awkward now that Ally wasn't there between them.

"I told you that you didn't know everything about me," Bree reminded him.

She could just blurt out the truth. Just spit out the words "Yes, I have a niece and she's your daughter," but she knew now was not the time. So instead, she changed the subject to something more comfortable. "I think we've finished cleaning up all of the backyard. Jared and Sky just hauled a truckload of limbs and leaves away. We just need to edge the sides of the driveway now."

Walking away, she grabbed a hoe one of the volunteers had brought out and began to work on one side of the driveway while Knox grabbed another tool and started on the other side. Together, they worked in silence. Soon, they were joined by some of the other staff members who had finished in the backyard. By the time they completed edging the drive, Jared and Sky were back and everyone began to fill the truck with the last of the yard trimmings. The junior Dr. Warner, Jared and his fiancée, Sky, left a few minutes later with the last truck full of leaves and limbs.

"I have to say I'm impressed with all the work that was done today," Knox said as he joined Bree as she headed to the backyard where the Legacy House mom, Maggie, had taken the volunteers' kids to play on the new equipment that had been donated for the children who sometimes came to stay with their moms.

"I'm impressed with Legacy House in general. Nashville is lucky to have a place like this.

It's nice to see that not only the office staff, but the community comes together to help the women here, too." Legacy House was truly a community project. There had been hundreds of women over the years who had found a safe haven there until they could find a permanent home.

"The news is so filled with the negatives of society, but I think that most people want to help others if they can. I see it a lot when I'm working in the rural areas up in the mountains. Neighbors help their neighbors, but most of them are just as willing to help out a stranger." Knox stopped and took a seat at an old picnic table that was in need of a coat of paint, something that one of the volunteers had mentioned needing to tackle on their next cleanup day at the house.

"It sounds exciting to work up in the mountains, never knowing what you are going to encounter, but what is it really like?" She was stalling, not wanting to leave without him getting to spend more time with Ally, while at the same time she'd wanted to ask him about his work in the mountains since the first time she'd heard of his work there.

"It's not like the TV shows. I'm not riding a horse up the side of the mountain every day, though I did ride one once with a local doctor who had an elderly woman that he wanted me to see. Her son had taken her down to the local clinic one day and when the doctor had recommended that she have surgery for a prolapsed uterus, she'd left swearing never to come see him again. He thought maybe with a second opinion, she'd change her mind. Needless to say, she took one look at the two of us and slammed the door."

"Well, that had to be discouraging," Bree said. While she'd worked with some difficult patients, she had never had one refuse to at least listen to what she had to say.

"It happens. Besides, I got a nice horse ride through some of the most beautiful country in the world," Knox said.

"You got to ride a horse?" Ally asked.

Bree hadn't realized the girl had come up beside her and was listening to their conversation. As Ally was getting older, Bree knew she needed to be more aware of what she said when her niece was around.

"I did. He was a really nice horse, too," Knox said as Ally came to sit beside him.

"Can I ride him?" Ally asked, moving closer to Knox.

"You can't ride that horse. He's not mine.

Besides, he lives a long way from here. But my parents have several horses at their ranch. If your parents are okay with it, maybe me and your aunt Bree can take you to see them."

"I don't have parents. I have Aunt Bree," Ally said before turning toward Bree. "Can we go see the horses?"

"We'll have to see," Bree said. Ally had always had a fascination with horses, even though she'd never been around one except for the ones at the county fair. And while she was happy that Knox and Ally had something to bond over now, taking Ally to Knox's parents' home? That came with complications she hadn't even considered. Not that she had anything against the couple. Bree had met them as a child. They both had been nothing but kind and encouraging to Bree and her sister when they were just starting out in their music career. But there was always the possibility that they would recognize Bree as one of the Rogers Sisters, wasn't there? Bree didn't think so. They'd only been twelve and she had changed a lot over those years. No longer was she the long-limbed, awkward little girl she'd been on those big, imposing stages. Still…

"That always means no," Ally said solemnly to Knox.

"I didn't say that…" Bree said, though the girl was right. Usually, it did mean the answer would be no.

"How about the three of us get something to eat together and we can talk about it then?" Knox asked, his eyes studying Bree.

Bree started to refuse; she could see that he had questions about Ally. He had to have figured out that she was raising Ally on her own. And the fact that she had never mentioned having a niece whom she was responsible for probably seemed strange, as if she had been hiding that fact. Of course, she had been. But explaining why might bring up questions she wasn't ready to answer. Not yet. She needed more time.

But still, this was an opportunity for them all to get to know each other. Wasn't that what she wanted? Didn't she need to see how Knox responded to having a child around?

"I think that would be great," she answered, surprising herself as much as her niece. "Where did you have in mind?"

Knox watched as Ally, Bree's niece, finished off her glass of chocolate milk. When the little girl looked up at him, a ring of chocolate circling her mouth, Knox thought she had to be the prettiest thing he had ever seen. With her aunt's strawberry blond hair and bright green eyes, Knox could have taken the child to be Bree's.

He couldn't understand why Bree had never mentioned that she was raising a child. Wasn't that something people just talked about? All the parents he knew couldn't talk about their children enough. He knew if he had a child, he'd probably be one of those parents, too. Was it because Bree wasn't the child's mother? He didn't think so. He'd observed Bree in her interactions with their patients at the clinic. She had always been warm and caring. So why did it seem that she had been keeping Ally a secret until today? She had told him that he didn't know everything about her. He had known that. After all, they'd only known each other for a short period of time. Still, this was something he thought would have come out at some point in their conversations together. If not at work, at least when they'd met at the bar. It would have explained one of the reasons she was working there. Supporting herself and a child while in school would have been tough.

"Can I have some money for the jukebox?" Ally asked.

Before Bree could open her purse, Knox

pulled out his wallet and handed her a five-dollar bill. "Do you want me to ask the lady at the register for change for the machine?"

"No, thank you. I can do it. I am eight years old, you know," the little girl said before turning and walking over to the counter where the waitress who had served their pizza stood.

"A little touchy about her age?" he asked Bree.

"Apparently, eight is the new twelve. At least, that seems to be what her and her friends think," Bree said, then sighed. "She's determined to grow up as fast as possible, while I just want the time to slow down so she can enjoy being a child for as long as possible."

"Weren't you like that? Eager to grow up? I know I was." It was just too bad that he had wasted so much of his life while he was growing up, making decisions that he wasn't old enough to make. He'd spent most of his teenage years rebelling against parents who had been too busy with their career to notice. He could only hope Ally wouldn't waste her childhood that way, because it was only later, when you grew up and looked back, that you realized what you had lost. But then Ally didn't have parents who were always gone on the road. It was easy to see the way that Bree interacted with her niece that the two of them were close.

"I guess I was," Bree said.

He watched as she stared into her half-empty glass. Was she thinking about mistakes she had made, just as he had? He knew so little about her, something that had never bothered him about other women. But whatever this fascination he had for Bree, it made him want to know everything. Even the tiny things. What was her favorite color? Her favorite movie? Did she even like movies? Maybe she preferred books. There was so much he wanted to know. "How did you end up with Ally? Did something happen to her parents?"

She looked at him for a moment, before her eyes dropped back to her drink. "Her mother, my sister, was injured in a car accident not long after Ally was born. She didn't survive. I've had Ally since she was a newborn."

"I'm sorry. That had to be hard." And explained so much, like the pain he'd seen in her eyes the night she'd sung at the bar. And that song. It had to be one she'd written about losing her sister. "So you've been raising her by yourself for eight years? It has to have been hard balancing school with raising a baby."

And Bree didn't have just school to worry about. She'd had to make a living, too. He knew she'd worked as a labor and delivery nurse; all midwives did at some point. Had she also been working at the bar then, too? "Where is her father? Doesn't he help you?"

"My sister…" Bree stopped midsentence and Knox could tell this wasn't something that was easy for her to talk about. He shouldn't have pushed her like he'd done.

"I'm sorry. It's none of my business. It's just that the thought of a man not supporting his daughter or the woman who had chosen to take care of his child, seems inexcusable to me."

"It's not like that," Bree said quickly. "It's complicated. My sister… Well, that's complicated, too."

"You don't have to tell me," Knox said. He didn't want Bree to feel like he was pressuring her to tell him all of her secrets, even though he wanted to know every single one.

"No, it's not that. I need to tell you this." Bree looked over to where Ally was picking out songs on the old-timey jukebox. "Ally's mother, my sister, she didn't feel that it would be a good thing for Ally's father to be involved in her daughter's life when she was born."

Knox didn't like the sound of that. "Was he abusive?"

"No, she never said that." Bree's voice sounded strange and he looked down to see her fingers had turned white as she gripped the table. "She just told me that he wouldn't want a baby and he would be a bad influence."

"So she never told him about the baby?" That didn't seem right to him. Didn't the man have a right to know? Even if he wasn't in a good place then, was it possible that knowing he had a child might have given him the encouragement to change?

"Look, I know it has to be hard talking about this. Your sister was young when you lost her, right?"

"She was my age," Bree said. "We were twins."

Twins. As an only child, he couldn't really appreciate what losing a sibling would be like, but it had to be hard. Losing a twin, someone you'd shared your whole life with, had to be even harder.

"Is it possible, then, that she might have changed her mind about Ally's father? Maybe they could have worked things out?" he said. "It just doesn't seem fair that he wasn't given that chance."

The small restaurant filled with music from

a well-known pop star as Ally rushed back over to them, cutting their conversation off.

Knox could see that Bree's niece was a happy, well-adjusted child, even after what had to be a rough start to her young life. He had no doubt it was because Ally had been lucky enough to have someone like Bree to take care of her.

And though it seemed wrong that Bree's sister hadn't told Ally's father about the pregnancy, it wasn't any of his business. It sounded as if the mother had been looking out for her child. What more could a parent do?

"Are you two talking about horses again?" Ally asked as she flung herself into the seat beside her aunt.

"No, we weren't. But if the invitation is still open, I think it would be a great idea for you to go see his parents' horses."

Knox was surprised by Bree's about-face on his invitation, but he wasn't about to lose the chance to spend more time with the two of them, as he was discovering that Ally was almost as enchanting as her aunt. "Are the two of you by any chance free tomorrow?"

That night, as Bree climbed into bed, she looked over to where a picture of her sister sat on her nightstand. Was she doing the right thing? Did she have a choice? She couldn't continue living with the knowledge of how her promise to her sister had affected Knox and Ally.

She picked up the picture of Brittany and a wave of grief hit her. How many nights had she cried herself to sleep while she was holding this picture? How long was she going to put herself through this? It was time to do the right thing for both Ally and Knox. And it was time to let go of the grief and guilt that she'd felt ever since Brittany had died.

She would always love and miss her sister. And even though they'd grown apart, Bree knew that Brittany had still loved her. Her sister wouldn't want her to keep going through this pain, night after night.

"I love you, Brittany," she said before setting the picture down, "and I'm sorry I have to break my promise to you, but I can't keep doing this. Ally deserves to know her father and Knox deserves to know his daughter."

Bree wiped away the tears from her eyes and took a shaky breath. "I will never forget you. You will always be my sister. But from now on, I'm going to concentrate on the good times we had, instead of what we lost. Because I deserve to be happy, too."

CHAPTER SIX

BY THE TIME Bree had gotten Ally ready for their trip to Knox's parents' ranch, her mind had come up with a dozen ways that what she was about to do could go wrong. What if Knox was so angry at her that he went to Dr. Warner and had her thrown out of the practice? What if his parents called one of their lawyers and had Ally taken away from her?

The doorbell sounded. It was too late to cancel now. Ally checked the door monitor as she'd been taught before skipping away to let Knox in. Bree rubbed her damp hands down her jeans. She had to make herself relax. She was doing the right thing.

Now that she'd cracked open a can of worms, she knew that it could be thrown wide open for the whole world to see by the end of that day. Scared of what might follow, she wanted to take her niece and hide in her closet. But she'd made her peace with her decision the night before. It was time for her to face Knox and tell him the truth.

Squaring her shoulders, she pasted a smile on her face as Knox walked inside, Ally beside him with her mouth going a hundred miles an hour.

"Sorry, she's been like this ever since she got up this morning," Bree said. "Ally, run and get your backpack."

As the girl ran off, twin pigtails flying behind her, Knox laughed. "She has a lot more energy than me at this time of the day."

"Me, too. Would you like a cup of coffee?" Bree asked, turning away from him and heading to the kitchen. She was finding it hard to look Knox in the eyes, something that didn't bode well for the rest of the day. She had to calm down. Trying to anticipate what his reaction to learning about Ally would be was too much. She just needed to take this one step at a time. The first thing to do was to get it over with, but there was no chance at that while Ally could interrupt them at any moment.

Right then, the little girl flew into the room. With eyes bright with excitement, she reminded Bree so much of Brittany right before she performed. It was pure, innocent joy on Ally's face, and Bree was so afraid she was about to destroy all of that if she didn't handle this right.

"Can we go now?" Ally begged, pulling on the leg of Knox's jeans.

"It looks like I'll need that coffee to go," Knox said, looking down at Bree's little girl, his own face just as happy-looking as the child's, before he looked back up at her.

With that one look, Bree's stomach unknotted and her body relaxed. Knox didn't even know that Ally was his child, yet Bree could see how much he enjoyed being around her. No matter how Knox took the news, as long as he loved Ally, it would be okay. Even though she knew that Bree and Knox's relationship would never be the same, it would all be worth it for Ally and Knox to have the life they deserved.

"Are we almost there?" Ally asked as Knox turned his truck down a small lane that led to his parents' ranch. She'd been asking the same question for the past thirty minutes, her excitement increasing with each mile.

"Almost. Keep looking over on your right and you might see a horse or two in the field," Knox said, then looked over at Bree. "I'm afraid of what she might do when she finally sees one of the horses."

"We had a talk about behaving around the horses this morning when she got up, but it would probably be a good idea for you to tell her, too." Bree wasn't really worried about Ally's safety. She knew that Knox wouldn't let her niece around any of the horses that were dangerous.

"I will. And I talked to the ranch manager, Rodney, about bringing the two of you out today. He was going to pick out a pony for Ally. I wouldn't take a chance with either of your safety."

"I know that," Bree said, and knew there was truth in his words. No matter what her sister had thought of Knox when he was younger, he wouldn't do anything to hurt Ally. Not intentionally at least.

Ally let out a squeal and began hopping up and down in her seat. "I see one, I see one."

Bree looked over to where her niece was pointing and saw a pretty brown-and-white horse standing in the field.

A few minutes later, they came to a halt in front of a large red metal barn. Before Bree could get out of the car, Ally had freed herself from her seat and was running toward it.

"Whoa, there," Knox said, catching up to Ally and stopping her, before taking a knee in front of her. "I know your aunt Bree told you that you needed to be careful around the horses. Running up to them is not being careful. You could spook one of them and they could hurt you or themselves."

"I don't want to hurt the horses," Ally said as her chin began to tremble, and big fat tears rolled down her cheeks.

Knox looked up at Bree with something akin to horror in his face. "I didn't mean to make her cry."

The man could handle all kinds of emergency situations in the operating room, but one little girl's tears scared him like this?

"It's okay, Ally. We know you don't want to hurt the horses. Knox just wants to make sure you are safe. And we did discuss no running around the horses this morning, didn't we?" Bree asked her niece.

"Yes, ma'am," Ally said, using her shirt-sleeve to wipe at her face before turning toward Knox. "I'm sorry, Dr. Knox. I won't run and scare the horses. I promise."

"That's okay," Knox said, standing and holding out a hand to Ally. "Let's go see some of my parents' horses. And then I have a surprise for you."

When Ally took Knox's hand, then looked

up at him with eyes full of trust, Bree's heart was filled with so much love that she felt as if it might burst out from her chest. She realized then that it wasn't just Ally she was feeling that love for, it was also for the man who held her niece's hand. How had her feelings for him changed so much, so fast? It was as if everything in the universe had thrown them together at just the perfect time.

"You coming?" Knox asked, looking back at her, then stopping as he studied her face. Did he see how much his simple act of taking her niece's hand in his had affected her? Could he see how much her own reaction to him was changing? Did he feel this way, too?

Not that it mattered. She couldn't make this about her and Knox. She had to remember that her focus had to be on Ally and Knox's relationship, not the way that her heart sped up every time he looked at her, just like the way he was looking at her now.

"Come on," he said, holding out his other hand to her. Was it wrong for her to wish everything could be different between them? That she could take what he offered her, the friendship and maybe more, without knowing that soon he might hate her for all the years of his daughter's life that she stole from him?

Unable to help herself, she reached out and took his hand. Its warmth calmed her. And for the next half hour she held on to it, wishing she would never have to let it go as he took them through the horse stables, pointing out one horse after another. Ally's excitement grew with each new horse they saw, but she stayed close to them as Knox had instructed her, while staff members went about their work hauling hay and cleaning the stalls.

"And this is where we keep my mother's ponies," Knox said when they got to the end of the stalls.

"Isn't your mom too big to ride a pony?" Ally asked as they stopped by an older man who was saddling up a small black pony.

"Mrs. Collins keeps the ponies around so that when little girls like you come over, you will be able to ride them," the man said, then removed his hat, exposing a bald head that was sporting a fresh sunburn, as he held out a hand for Bree to shake. "I'm Rodney, ma'am."

Letting go of Knox's hand, she took the man's hand, noting its rough callouses that reminded her of her father's. "It's nice to meet you, Rodney. I'm Bree. And this is Ally."

"It's nice to meet you both. This here is

Sammy. He's a nice little pony that likes little girls. Do you want to pet him, Ally?"

With a nod from Bree, Ally approached the pony slowly, before placing her hand on the top of its head like Rodney showed her.

"I think it's love at first sight," she whispered to Knox when he stepped closer.

"I think so, too," he said. But when she looked up at him, she noticed that it was she he was looking at, instead of her niece. Her hand shook when his hand reached down for hers again. She let him take it. Why couldn't she enjoy a few moments before everything came crashing down around her?

They stood and watched Ally get her first lesson on how to saddle the pony before Rodney helped her up onto the pony's back and led her out of the barn and into an adjoining paddock.

"There you are." A loud feminine voice came from behind them. Turning, Bree saw Gail Collins approaching. The years since Bree had seen her had been good to her. Though there was a little gray in the woman's long dark blond hair, her face carried very few wrinkles. Dressed in jeans and sporting a rhinestone belt buckle, she still looked like the Country Music

Queen she'd been all those years ago when Bree had met her.

"Bree, this is my mom," Knox said as the beautiful woman stretched up on her toes and planted a noisy kiss on his cheek. Instead of shrugging off her attention, Knox wrapped his free arm around her. "Mom, this is Bree Rogers. She's the midwife who has been working with me at the county clinic."

"It's nice to meet you, Bree," Knox's mother said before stepping back and studying Bree. "Have we met before?"

Bree knew that this time would come. She was bound to meet Knox's mother someday. Yet, she still hadn't decided on how to handle it. With the exception of telling Knox about Ally, she had always stuck to the truth. It seemed best to do that now. "Yes, ma'am, but I doubt you'd remember me. I was only twelve years old at the time. My sister and I used to perform when we were kids. We were known as the Rogers Sisters."

"I remember now. The two of you were twins, not identical, though you did look similar."

"It was the hair and eyes," Bree said, shooting a look over at Knox, waiting for him to put the two things together. Hadn't Brittany told him about her childhood career?

"And you're a midwife now?" the woman said, still studying her.

"Yes, ma'am. I'm just finishing up my residency now."

"And your sister?" Knox's mother asked. "Did she leave the business, too?"

"Mom, Bree's sister was killed right after her daughter, Bree's niece, was born," Knox said, cutting into what was starting to feel like an inquisition. "That's the little girl, Ally, that I told you I was bringing to see the horses. We were just about to walk outside so we could watch Rodney work with Ally. He has her on Sammy."

"I'm so sorry, Bree. Please excuse me from asking so many questions. It's just so rare for Knox to bring a woman out here to meet us. I just want to know all about you. And it's so interesting that we met when you were a child."

Bree looked over at Knox and caught him rolling his eyes at his mother's statement. His mother changed the subject to ponies and horses, then circled back to her hopes that someday she would have grandchildren to teach to ride all the horses she'd collected. Bree wanted to laugh at the woman's not so subtle hints that Knox needed to get busy in the baby-making department.

But once they reached the paddock, the woman stopped talking and just stared where Ally sat on the pony, listening carefully to every word Rodney said. Never had Bree seen her niece look so serious.

"She's beautiful, Bree," Knox's mother said from behind her. "And a natural in the saddle. Look how perfectly she's seated. She'll make a great rider."

Bree didn't know what to say to that, so she just stood there, still holding Knox's hand, and watched as her niece took one more step away from her into a life that Bree would never be able to give her.

Fifteen minutes later, she could see that Ally was getting tired. Fortunately, Gail Collins could see it, too. "Let me go get her back to the stable."

When Bree started to follow her, Knox pulled her aside. "I'm sorry if my mother upset you with her questions about your sister. She didn't mean to."

"I know that. She had no way of knowing," Bree said, wanting to say so much more. She suddenly needed to get all of this off her chest, once and for all. Both Knox's and his mother's kindness was just too much. She didn't deserve any of it.

She pulled her hand from his, feeling the loss immediately. Then she wrapped her arms around herself, unexpectedly cold while in the warmth of the summer sun.

"I need to talk to you. Privately." The words sounded more ominous than she'd meant them to and the whole mood of the day changed as Knox looked at her, his eyes worried.

"I asked my mother to have a picnic fixed for the two of us. I thought I could show you some of the ranch and I know my mom would love to spend time with Ally. That is, if you would like that," Knox said as they walked back into the stable where they were greeted by a smiling Ally and Knox's mother.

"Ms. Gail says I can come to her house and see her horse collection," Ally said. "They aren't real horses, but she says some of them have pink and purple ribbons I can braid in their hair."

"That sounds like a lot of fun. But you have to be careful and not break them," Bree told her niece.

"I'll run in and get the food. Then we can go down to the pond," Knox said. "Or you can come up to the house with me if you would like."

Bree followed him out of the barn where she could see the two-story house that stood to the north. It was a beautiful house. And just one more thing to remind her that Knox and his parents could give Ally so much more than she could.

Around her, the fields of grass swayed with the summer breeze. Even with the voices of the workers in the stables, there was a calming quietness there that she needed. "No, I'll wait here."

She strode over to a fencerow and placed one boot-clad foot on the first fence post she came to, welcoming this short period of time she had alone with her thoughts. She was going to do this. She had no other choice. Even without seeing her niece walk off, hand in hand with the grandmother she had never known, Bree knew coming clean with Knox about Ally had to be done now. Her and Ally's time alone together was up.

It was only a few minutes before she heard the sound of a small motor headed her way. She turned to see Knox driving an all-terrain cart toward her, a basket sitting beside him.

"Climb in," Knox said when he stopped and moved the basket to the back floorboard.

Bree took the seat beside him, buckling herself in before Knox started down the drive. He then took a right turn down a worn path through an open field running beside another paddock, this one larger with a taller fence.

She grabbed a handle above her as they drove over the rocky path at a speed that at first scared her, then became thrilling. By the time they had arrived by a large pond, they both were laughing.

For a moment, Bree forgot that she was about to spill a secret that would change all their lives. When Knox bent his head toward hers, she knew she should stop him, but she couldn't find the strength to turn her head away. As his lips brushed against hers in a gentle kiss, she closed her eyes and made a wish for her and Knox to someday get a second chance. When she opened her eyes, she found Knox's face still close to hers. Her hand cupped his cheek, the day's stubble rough against her skin.

"Something's bothering you, Bree. Is it those questions from my mom? She didn't mean to bring up bad memories," Knox said, his eyes watching her with an intensity she'd never experienced. It wasn't the first time she'd seen him like this. It was as if he was memorizing everything about her in that moment. As if he wanted to sink into her soul and know all her secrets.

And now he was about to learn more than he could ever have imagined.

"It's not that, not really. I've decided that instead of thinking about those bad memories, I need to concentrate on the good ones. Over the years, I've let the loss of my sister define our relationship, and I shouldn't have. Does that make sense?" She didn't know why she was telling him this, but it seemed important that he understand that she was making changes in her life. Looking at things differently. Just like she was looking at him differently now.

"It makes a lot of sense. Everybody handles the grieving process in different ways and in different time frames. But if that isn't what's bothering you, what is it?"

"Can we have just a few more minutes before I tell you?"

"Of course we can," Knox said, moving away from her and reaching over for the basket. When she joined him, he took her hand and led her down to where a weather-beaten wood pier had been built across part of the pond. When they got to the end of the pier, he put the basket down, then sat down beside it. Hanging his feet over the end of the pier, he offered Bree a hand and she took a seat beside him before looking out at the lake with its mirror-smooth surface. It was the calm before the storm.

Opening the basket, Knox pulled out sandwiches and drinks, laying them between them, along with some fruit. Her stomach was queasy, but she forced herself to unwrap a sandwich and take a bite. She wasn't sure if her stomach was reacting to her nerves about what she was about to do or if it was because of the kiss they'd just shared.

They ate in silence as they both looked out across the water. A fish hit the top of the water startling Bree and causing her to jump and let out a nervous laugh. The hollowness of it seemed to echo across the lake.

"I don't know where to start. I know I should start at the beginning, but I can't say I even know where this all began. Maybe you can help me with that."

"I'd be glad to help you if I can," Knox said, turning toward her, laying his sandwich down. "Maybe if you tell me what's wrong, the two of us can fix it."

Bree looked at him sitting there beside her. He was so calm. So reassuring. It was hard to believe he was the same man that her sister had been so adamant that he wouldn't be good for her child.

Bree had made such a big mistake all those years ago, not giving him a chance to prove that he would be a good father.

"I'm going to tell you everything I know, and then maybe you can help fill in some of the blanks for me. You see, before my sister died, I hadn't heard from her in over eighteen months even though we lived in the same city."

"I'm sorry to hear that. Families can be so complicated," Knox said. "But I don't know where I come in."

"I know you don't. And that's my fault, not yours. I should have told you this months ago." She looked away from him then, seeking the calm she'd felt from their surroundings earlier, but it didn't come. Maybe she didn't deserve it. Maybe she deserved all the sleepless nights, and guilty nerves she'd suffered for the past few weeks. "No. That's not right. I should have told you this years ago. But I didn't know you then. And I'd made a promise I didn't think I could break."

When Knox started to interrupt her, she rested a hand on his chest. "Do you even remember my sister?"

* * *

Knox stared at Bree. She was talking in circles, making it impossible to figure out what it was that she was trying to tell him. Her sister? Why would he remember her sister?

"She had dyed her hair, it was more red than blond the last time I saw her, but she would still have had my eyes. She still went by her first name, Brittany. But she had changed her last name to Moore. She didn't want people to remember her from our childhood performance."

The name was vaguely familiar, but why? Then it hit him. "She was working at one of the recording studios as a backup singer. I remember her. She hung out with some of the music crowd I knew. I didn't know her that well…" A memory surfaced then. Red hair. Beautifully haunting green eyes. It was the night he and Thad had been out partying. She had been with the group of his parents' band members whom Knox had stayed back with when Thad had left the bar. As it always did, thoughts of Thad brought back all his old grief and guilt. He talked a good talk with Bree about grieving, but he was still struggling himself with the loss of his friend.

And the girl? He remembered meeting her at the bar that night, and then the two of them sharing a car ride. Later, at his place, they had shared more. Was that what this was all about? Did Bree know that her sister had spent the night with him? "She went by Britt," he said. "I guess like the way you go by Bree, instead of Brianna."

"She did go by Britt, sometimes. It was usually only with people she was close to, though," Bree said, her eyes looking at him expectantly, like he had the answer to a question he didn't know.

Or was she just waiting for him to admit that he had slept with her sister? His life then had been so different. He'd lived it one day at a time, never thinking about the consequences. That is, until the night Thad was killed.

"I don't know what your sister told you, but back then, when I met your sister, I wasn't the same person I am now. I was young and reckless. There are a lot of things I wish I had done differently then. I'm sorry if the night I spent with your sister upsets you. It's not something I'm proud of." Revisiting that night was a nightmare. He and Thad had started partying early that day and hadn't had the good sense to stop. If it hadn't been for who his parents were, he was sure the bars would have thrown them out on the streets.

But then, if his parents hadn't been who they were, he might not have acted out the way he had. It hadn't been until he reached rock bottom that he and his parents had realized how unhealthy their relationship had become. Thank goodness they'd been able to work things out then, before there was any more damage to their relationship.

But that night had been before he'd come to his senses. He could barely remember the girl he now knew as Bree's sister, offering to get him home. It wasn't until that morning when he'd received the call that Thad was in the hospital with little hope of surviving, that Knox had finally sobered up. He'd left Bree's sister in his bed without an explanation and hadn't returned until the next night. He was ashamed to say that he hadn't given Brittany another thought, until now.

It was like all his sins were coming back to revisit him when he looked over at Bree. How did he tell her that he'd known her sister, but all she'd meant to him was one night of drunken pleasure?

"I don't know what your sister told you about me. I can tell you that I'm not the man I was then and I'm ashamed of the way I acted that night. I wish I could say that there weren't any more women like her, one-night stands with women I barely knew, but I can't. I can use my youth as an excuse, but I don't want to make excuses. I learned the hard way that you have to take responsibility for your actions and face the consequences. I did that many years ago, but sometimes those consequences last for years."

"I don't understand. Are you saying that Brittany was just a one-night stand? Because that isn't how she acted. She acted like the two of you had been together and it had ended badly. I took it to mean that the two of you were involved."

Knox looked over at Bree. Her face was pale, her pupils almost pinpoint. She looked as if she was in shock as she stared at him. Gone was the warmth he was used to seeing in her eyes. She looked like she'd seen a ghost. The ghost of her sister? Because right then he felt like Brittany was standing there between the two of them.

How did he fix this without making it look like he was calling her sister a liar? Had he said something that would have made Brittany think that there was more between the two of them? How could that even be possible when he'd never seen her again?

After Thad's death, he'd applied himself to

finishing his exams. And when the guilt and depression from Thad's death had threatened to send him back into his bad ways, he'd checked himself into a rehab. He'd cut all ties then, only taking calls from his parents until he'd found the help he needed to get his life onto a path he was proud of.

"I'm sorry, Bree. I don't want to hurt you or suggest that Brittany wasn't truthful, but the only thing that me and Brittany shared was one night together. That was all."

Knox started to gather the leftover meal wrappers. This was not the way he had planned for the two of them to end the day. When Bree's hand closed over his as he reached for the last of their mostly uneaten meal, he looked up at her, expecting to see anger, disgust, or the coolness she'd treated him to the first months they'd worked together.

But there was none of those things. Instead, there was sorrow and regret. "But that wasn't all you shared, Knox. The two of you shared Ally."

CHAPTER SEVEN

THERE WAS NO laughing on their ride back to the ranch house, as Knox shot off question after question at her. Bree couldn't blame him for the anger she could see brewing in his eyes.

"How is that possible?" he asked, then shook his head when she didn't answer. He was an OB/GYN; he knew how pregnancy happened as well as she did.

"Okay, let's say I am Ally's father. Why wouldn't Brittany have told me?" he asked, then answered the question himself before she could answer. "She would have found out about the pregnancy when I was away in rehab. I didn't have my phone with me. Only my parents knew how to contact me. But after? When Ally was born? I would have been out then. She should have called then."

"I told you I had a lot of blanks I needed you to fill in. I only talked to her the once in eighteen months. She hadn't told me anything about the pregnancy. I don't have any proof of this, but I've always thought that she might have been considering giving up Ally. Maybe that's why she didn't tell either of us? Maybe it wasn't until Ally was born that she decided to keep her. We've both seen that happen before."

Knox swerved around a rock in the middle of the path, causing Bree to grip the over-the-head handle even tighter.

"Maybe we should stop." He'd been driving full throttle since he'd insisted that they get back to the ranch as soon as possible. He was upset. Shocked. But so was she.

Learning that her assumption that Brittany and Knox had been involved in a relationship was wrong changed everything. What if Ally wasn't even Knox's child? She hadn't been able to say those words out loud, but he had to be thinking them, too.

Was it possible? Could it be that Brittany had made that part of her story up, too? The answer to that question tore Bree in two. On one hand, if Knox wasn't Ally's father, Bree could let go of the guilt she'd felt at assuming that he wasn't fit to be. And if Knox wasn't Ally's father, she wouldn't have to worry about losing Ally. On the other hand, that would mean that there was another man out there who could someday challenge Bree for her niece. A man who wouldn't be as kind and caring as Knox. A man who might not be good for her niece.

Being honest with herself, Bree knew that Ally having Knox for a father would be good for her. And she had to admit that it would be best if her niece's paternity was settled sooner instead of later.

Knox stopped the cart, but he didn't look at her. "We need a plan. We can't tell my mother this. And I know we can both agree that we can't tell Ally until we know for sure that I'm her father. There's places in Nashville that can run a paternity test in a day. We need to get that done first." He turned his head to her, his eyes somber now. "And then we need to have a long talk, no matter what the results."

The rest of their time at the ranch seemed to fly by as Knox did everything but rush them out to his truck. She started to stop him and ask if he thought she was going to just blurt out the news that Ally was his child to his mother or if he just couldn't stand to be around her anymore, but she was afraid to hear his answer.

He was angry and confused. She got that. She was, too. Just like him, she wanted to know the truth about her niece.

And she was also afraid. Only this time it

wasn't the fear that she'd spoken to Lucretia about, the fear of losing Ally. This was a new fear. Something she was ashamed to admit because it was so selfish of her. What right did she have to fear that what she and Knox had begun to feel for each other had been destroyed when he was now faced with the fact that he had trusted her and she had betrayed him by not sharing Brittany's secret with him?

By the time Knox dropped her and Ally off at their home, Bree had come to accept that there was little hope that Knox would forgive her, even if Ally wasn't his child. There had to be trust in any relationship, especially one as new as theirs. She could try to make excuses for her actions all day long, but the man who'd driven them home without even looking at her once was not going to listen to them. And she couldn't blame him.

The new week started off with a stop by a local lab where Bree could pick up a DNA paternity test. She had asked Knox to let her explain to Ally, but Bree still didn't know how to do that. While Bree believed in being truthful, she didn't think her niece was old enough to understand DNA or what it was used for. She'd finally decided in the middle of the night that it was best, for now, to just tell Ally it was a test she needed.

The rest of the day had gone by quickly with Bree and Lori attending two deliveries, one of which Bree was primary. The good thing about being busy was that it didn't give her a lot of time to think about her own problems. She'd only seen Knox once in the clinic hallway, but they'd both been too busy to stop and talk.

It wasn't until the next day, after she'd carefully swabbed Ally's cheek then dropped her off at school, that Bree had time to worry about the outcome of the paternity test. When she walked into the county clinic, she went straight to the back office and took the safely packaged test from her backpack. Knowing she could trust Lucretia not to snoop, she put the test in a paper bag and added a note to let Knox know it was for him.

A few minutes later, Knox stopped by Lucretia's desk where she and Bree were discussing supply list changes. After nodding his head toward the exam rooms, Bree followed him. He handed her the paper bag that contained the test, and she slipped it into her pocket. She couldn't help but smile at the way they were treating this.

"I feel like I should have a hat and fake mustache. Maybe a trench coat, too," Bree said, hoping that she could lighten up the situation.

"I'd like to see you in a trench coat," Knox said, surprising Bree with the teasing comeback before turning serious again. "How did it go with Ally? She ask anything about the test?"

"Not at all. I admit I was surprised. I wasn't sure what I was going to say if she asked me what the test was for. I've always been honest with her about everything, but sometimes you can't tell someone everything you want to. Sometimes things are more complicated than the simple truth."

"If you are talking about your not telling me about Ally, I know there were reasons you didn't tell me. You made a promise to your sister, and then she passed away. But I don't understand how, after you met me, after you saw that I wasn't a bad person, you didn't tell me then. Why, Bree? Didn't you think I deserved to know if Ally was my child?"

How could she make him understand the weight of her sister's secret that she had carried for years? How could she expect him to forgive her for not telling him? "It was the last thing I told her, Knox. The last thing I said to my sister. I promised her that I wouldn't tell anyone about who was Ally's father."

She walked the length of the small exam room, then turned and started back to him. "Until this weekend I had never broken that promise. I had held my sister's secret deep inside and never dreamed of telling anyone the truth about Ally. Until I met you. And though I'm not proud of it, if you had been the type of man Brittany had accused you of being, I wouldn't have told you then. The only person I had ever considered telling Brittany's secret to was Ally when she got old enough to make her own decisions about the information her mother had given me."

"So, what? When she was eighteen or nineteen, she'd have suddenly showed up on my doorstep? Would that have been fair to either of us?" Knox asked, coming to stand in the path where she had been pacing the floor.

"Nothing about this situation is fair to any of us," Bree said, stopping in front of him. "It wasn't fair that Brittany was killed in an accident before she had the chance to raise her child. Who knows? Maybe once she had Ally at home, she would have changed her mind. But we'll never know that, will we?"

"You're right," Knox said, running his hands through his hair where it had fallen down in front of his face. "This hasn't been fair for anyone."

Bree heard a door shut and then Lucretia talking to someone who would be their first patient of the day. Holding the brown paper bag up in front of her, she nodded at Knox. "But at least with this we will have the truth."

Because until they found out if Knox was really Ally's father, there was no way for them to move forward.

Bree rushed back to put the test in her backpack before following Knox to the front of the office to greet their patient. By the time Bree got there, other patients had begun to file into the waiting room. The little office was soon full again, as it had been every day that Bree had been there. While Bree was glad to be busy, she hated that there were so many women who couldn't afford to get care. They provided what they could, but it wasn't the same.

For her last appointment of the day, Lucretia brought back a woman in her midthirties, along with an elderly woman whose eyes darted around the room, taking everything in. "This is Leah and her grandmother."

"It's nice to meet you both. What brings you to the clinic today?" Bree asked, still watching the older woman who was acting uneasy.

"My grandmother, Camila, she doesn't speak English. She has a knot, a lump, in her breast. I don't know where to take her to get this looked at. My sister says she needs a mammogram, but where do we get this?" The younger woman looked at Bree with worried eyes and Bree instantly understood her concerns.

Bree had lost her own mother to breast cancer. If her mother had gone to get her yearly exam, the cancer would have been caught earlier and her mother might still be alive today. "If it's okay with you and your grandmother, I'd like to give her an exam. That way we can make sure there isn't any other issue that we need to investigate. Then I'll get a mammogram scheduled."

After giving the woman a thorough exam, Bree left them in the exam room while she went to find Lucretia. She knew that there were programs run by the local hospitals to help women get their yearly mammogram, but she wasn't sure where the information was.

"I'm glad you're here," Lucretia said when Bree stepped into the reception office. "There's someone outside the office pacing back and forth. I think it's that young girl. The teenager from last week."

Bree stepped into the waiting room and

looked out the door. She could see the shadow of someone outside the frosted door, standing against the back wall of the hallway. It was possible that it was someone waiting for a patient to finish, maybe another grandchild of Camila's, but Bree didn't think so. She'd waited all day for the frightened girl who had run away to come back. Bree was pretty sure that she had.

Bree went over to the reception window. She didn't want to let the girl get away before she could talk to her, but she also didn't want Leah or Camila to think she had forgotten about them. "Can you find the information for the free mammogram programs at the hospital and make an appointment for the patient in my exam room? Her granddaughter has all her contact information. It could be benign, but there is definitely a large mass in her right breast that needs to be seen to immediately. I'm going to ask Knox to recommend a surgeon who will work with them on finances once we get the results of the mammogram back."

"I can do that," Lucretia said. "What are you going to do?"

"I'm going to see if it's our returning patient. If it is, I'm not going to let her get away this time." Bree started toward the door. "Don't let anyone else out this door until I tell you to."

"Maybe we should call the police? What if she's dangerous? She pushed you over last time she was here," Lucretia said, leaning over the reception window.

"She's not dangerous. She was just scared."

"Wait," Lucretia said, holding out a pack of peanut butter crackers, "take these."

"You're the best," Bree told Lucretia, taking the crackers and heading back to the door. Maybe if she couldn't talk the girl into coming inside, she could bribe her.

She opened the door and stepped into the hallway, leaving the door open for a second while she waited to see what the girl's reaction was. Bree had denied to Lucretia that the girl was dangerous, but what did she really know about her? Fear made people do things that they normally wouldn't do. It had certainly caused Bree to make some bad decisions.

When the girl didn't run, Bree closed the door behind her, then held out the crackers. Once again, Bree noted the fear in the girl's eyes. "We thought you might like these."

The girl stared at the simple package of crackers like it was steak and lobster before looking at Bree with suspicion. "It's okay. They're for you."

"What do I have to do for them?" the girl

asked, her young face transforming from that of a child's to a hardened adult in seconds. Bree had no doubt now that this girl was being abused in some way.

"You don't have to do anything," Bree said, coming to stand against the wall across from the girl. She wanted to take the girl into her arms and promise her she'd keep her safe, but that would only frighten the girl more. "You don't even have to talk to me if you don't want to."

When the girl reached for the crackers, Bree leaned forward toward her, then moved back away from her again. She wanted to cry when she saw the girl rip open the package of crackers and stuff the first one into her mouth. She wanted to go inside the office and get more for the girl to eat, but she was still afraid the girl would bolt on her.

When the girl finished the crackers and didn't run, Bree decided to take a chance. At some point someone was going to have to come out the office door and she didn't know how the girl would react. "Do you want something to drink? We have all kinds of bottled drinks inside. I can get you one if you don't want to come inside."

The girl's head shot up at the mention of a drink, her eyes coming to rest on the office door. Bree could tell that she wanted to go inside. The girl had come there for help. Bree just had to find a way to make her feel safe. "My name is Bree. I just started here as a midwife in training, but I can tell you that this is a safe place. No one is going to make you do anything you don't want to do here. But if you need help, you've come to the right place. We help people with all kinds of problems and we keep everything confidential. It's what we do."

"I'm Christine," the girl said, barely above a whisper, her voice sounding raw as if she hadn't used it in a while.

"Well, Christine, do you want to come inside with me? I don't mind talking in the hallway, but our office would be more private." When the girl didn't move, Bree continued. "I know you're scared. That's okay. I've been scared, too. Sometimes trusting someone is the scariest thing of all."

The girl pushed away from the wall, then stood staring at Bree. They stood there looking at each other for almost a minute, before big fat tears began to run down the girl's face and her body began to shake. "My name isn't

Christine. That's the name the people who took me told me to use. My real name is Megan. Megan Johnson, and all I want is to go home. Can you help me?"

Knox walked out of an exam room where he had been speaking with the police officers that had been called when Bree had come inside with a sobbing teenager who had begun to spill her story. It had only taken a few minutes for him to realize they were dealing with a victim of human trafficking and they needed more help than he and Bree knew how to give. Once Megan had gone into the back with Lucretia, who had been happy to play momma hen to the young girl, they'd made the call to the police.

"They've contacted Megan's mother in Memphis and she's headed to the downtown Nashville police station," Knox said when he pulled Bree into the hallway.

"I know. I talked to her mother after Megan talked to her. She needs to be taken to a hospital for an exam, but I haven't been able to bring myself to mention that yet. She's so fragile right now, Knox. Her mother says this was the first time she had run away. The first time she's done anything like that. They had a fight about a boy who had been hanging around the park where she skateboarded." Bree took a deep breath before she looked up at Knox with what could only be described as murder in her eyes. "The boy was a twenty-two-year-old man who was hooked up with other human traffickers. It was all a setup."

Knox's arm came around Bree as her whole body shook with anger. "She's only seventeen. She should feel safe to go to the park and skateboard."

Knox was afraid that the young girl might never feel safe again. "From what the officers told me, it sounds like Megan's mother will make sure she gets the help she needs."

One of the officers came out from where she had gone to talk to the young girl and handed both him and Bree a card. "We're going to take Megan downtown to meet with our human trafficking officers. She's got a lot of information that they will find helpful. She's willing to talk with them, but she wants Ms. Lucretia to go along with her. The team might have questions for you, too."

Knox, along with Bree, offered to help in any way they could. While Bree went to say goodbye to Megan and help Lucretia gather her things, Knox pulled the officer over to the side. "Is there any chance that someone followed her here? Do I need to worry about the safety of the office?"

"That's one of the reasons I gave you my card. From what Megan says, she was sent here by one of the traffickers to obtain birth control pills. If you see anything suspicious, please call."

The officer's words made Knox feel sick. He hoped that the information Megan had would help to put the traffickers away, where they belonged. If not, there'd be another girl, in another park, and that one might not have the courage to do what Megan had done.

The young girl came down the hall, Lucretia following close behind her. When the girl hesitated at the door, one of the officers got in front of her while the other followed behind them. Bree pressed a note in the girl's hand before the officer opened the door and they walked out.

"What was that?" he asked.

"I gave her my number, in case she needs something. Or if she just wants to talk." A beeper on Bree's phone went off. "I'm running behind. Ally went home with a friend today, but I don't want to be late picking her up."

Knox watched her reach into her pocket and pull out the bag holding the paternity test. "Can you drop this off for me?"

Knox reached for the bag and Bree's hand closed around his.

"I can't imagine what Megan's mother is feeling right now. She's been going through hell for two weeks wondering if her daughter was even alive. I know we have a lot going on right now, but the most important thing is Ally is safe. And I know no matter what happens with these results, she'll still be safe."

"You're right. No matter what happens with these results," Knox said, "there is nothing more important than that Ally stays safe."

CHAPTER EIGHT

BREE LISTENED TO Ally chatter about her day at school as she began to mix the pancake batter. With only two more days left before summer break, Ally and her friends were getting more and more excited with plans for their time off. Bree, on the other hand, was already worried about how she was going to get someone to watch Ally on the nights she and Lori took call at the hospital. But most of all Bree was worried about the email that she had received from the lab that afternoon with the results of the paternity test.

"Is Knox going to be here soon?" Ally asked again. Ever since Bree had told her niece that she had invited Knox over for pancakes, the little girl had run back and forth from the front window to the kitchen.

Bree looked at the clock on the stove; she was getting anxious, too. Knowing that the information in the email could change both of their lives, she kept glancing over at her laptop as if the thing could open itself and spew out the information. Not that she was ready for the results on the paternity test.

While she wanted to know the truth about Ally's father, Bree knew that it could change everything about her and Ally's life. Knox had made it clear that his priority was Ally, but what did that really mean?

Bree looked around the tiny house that she had made into a home for her and Ally. It wasn't even theirs. She had been renting it month to month, not knowing where she would be settling once she got her midwifery certification. Would Knox see all the work and the love for Ally that she had put into the home? Or would he see the tiny, outdated place as something not good enough for the granddaughter of Gail and Charles Collins? He'd been brought up on a ranch that was bigger than the whole suburb where Bree had grown up.

Ally had just rushed back into the room when the doorbell finally rang. Jumping up and down with more energy than she should have had that late in the day, her niece raced back toward the door. "I've got it."

Bree forced herself not to run to the door alongside her niece. She told herself that she was anxious to see Knox because she was anxious to read the email with him. But she had been just as excited to see him every time they had passed in the halls of the Legacy Clinic that day. Something had changed between them since the day she had shared with him the truth about Ally. For the first time there had been no secrets between the two of them. She'd admitted her guilt and her fears and he'd admitted his own struggles when he was younger. If the two of them didn't have the results of the paternity test hanging over them, Bree thought that maybe the two of them might have had a chance to find something deeper.

But those results could be the very thing that destroyed that chance.

"Look what Dr. Knox brought," Ally said as Knox followed her into the kitchen carrying a large carton of chocolate milk, along with a bottle of wine.

"Is the chocolate milk for me?" Bree asked him, then looked down to Ally.

"He said it's for me, but you can have a glass," Ally said, reaching for it.

Bree turned back to the stove and began to pour the batter on the griddle. "It will definitely go with your dinner."

"It's Wednesday, so it's pancake night. Do

you like pancakes?" Ally asked as she and Knox took a stool at the counter.

"I love pancakes. My mom's cook, Ms. Jenkins, makes them for breakfasts whenever I spend the night at my parents' house."

"You don't live with your mom?" Ally asked before jumping down and running over to where the dishes were kept.

"No. I have a house of my own. Like your aunt Bree."

Ally came back with the dishes and then ran back to get the utensils, explaining, "It's my job to set the table. Aunt Bree says we have to share the chores."

"That sounds like a good plan. Sharing is important," Knox said, his tone as serious as her niece's.

"So I guess the two of you can share these pancakes," Bree said as she took two plates and put a pancake on each of them. She placed bacon from the pile she had cooked earlier on each plate then brought them back to the counter. "This should get you started."

Bree listened to their conversation as she finished, then went to sit beside them at the kitchen counter that also acted as their dining table. Occasionally, she would join in, but mostly she just listened, enjoying the sound of her niece's laughter and the patience in which Knox answered all the little girl's questions.

It would have been a perfect meal if she didn't have the DNA test results weighing on her. She forced each bite of pancake down to her nervous stomach, until it protested.

"I'll do the dishes," Knox said when the last pancake had been eaten.

"You don't have to do that," Bree protested. "You're our guest tonight."

"And sometimes guests help with dishes. It's sharing, right, Ally?"

'I can help, too," Ally said as she started to take the dishes off the counter and carry them to the sink.

"Me and Knox will do the dishes. You need to go take a shower and get ready for bed," Bree said, preparing herself for the child's nightly complaints when it came to bedtime.

"Can we read tonight?" Ally asked.

"We'll see. Remember last night you took too long in the shower and we didn't have time to read." And Bree had felt guilty because it had been she who had been too tired to read that night, not Ally.

It seemed every day was getting shorter and shorter. Each night she climbed into bed making a list of everything she needed to accomplish the next day, but it didn't seem as if she ever caught up. Between working at the two clinics, taking care of Ally and then working weekends at the bar, she never had a moment free. Add in the sleepless nights where she went from scared of what would happen with the results of the paternity to fanciful dreams of Knox kissing her again, and she was emotionally and physically drained.

"She'll be in there a while if you want us to check the email," Bree said, taking a plate from Knox and adding it to the sink.

"How about we wait until after we get these done?" Knox said as he picked up a towel.

"It's okay if you're nervous," Bree said. "I know I am."

"I'm not nervous, I'm terrified," Knox said. "Part of me wants to know the truth, while the other part worries that I'm not ready for it."

"Why is that?" she asked, though she could understand how he felt. She wanted to ask him then what his plans would be if Ally was his, while at the same time she didn't want to know what he would say.

Because unlike Knox, she was already convinced she knew what the results would be. Her sister might have changed over the last years while they'd been apart, but she didn't think

Brittany would have lied about her baby's father. Why would she lie to Bree? It wouldn't have made sense.

"I'm just afraid of messing things up. My parents weren't always the best. They had a lot going on with their careers when they had me. I felt I was just an afterthought sometimes. They mostly hired staff to take care of me instead of spending time with me themselves. I'm not blaming them. The music business is rough to break in to, as I'm sure you already know. Once you get to the top, it's even harder to remain there. They did the best they could, I'm sure…"

While he said the words convincingly enough, she wasn't sure how much of it he truly believed. Families were complicated. She and her sister were a good example of that.

"I think fame and fortune change people. I know my mom changed her whole focus on life from being my mom to being me and Britt's manager. I would never want that for my child. I missed the mom I had before, the one who cared more about my everyday life than about whether I'd sung that note perfectly in practice." Bree paused with a half-washed dish in her hand, then let out a short laugh. "Don't I sound so high and mighty. The truth is, it's a struggle every day to keep my focus on Ally. I've spent most of her life working weekends to pay the bills and attending classes during the week. Some days I wonder if it was worth all the time I've missed with her. Even when I had a couple years of working in the hospital before I started midwifery school, I was working extra to pay off my college loans."

"I've seen how the two of you get along. Ally knows she's an important part of your life. You two are like a team. That's something special. I wish I'd had that with my parents. I think that's one of the reasons that my mom wants grandchildren so badly. She wants to do it right this time. And if I'm Ally's father, I want to do it right the first time. I don't want to look back like she does and see I did all the wrong things. I'll already be starting out behind."

"When Ally was born, I was only twenty-one. Suddenly, I had a baby to look after and a funeral to plan. I was drowning in grief while also trying to figure out my new life. But then one night I looked down at Ally and saw her looking up at me. I promised her then that I would be the best aunt I could be. I haven't been perfect, Knox, I know that. But I want you to know that I've always done my best."

She turned off the water and dried her hands.

"I don't know how this is going to work out. If you aren't Ally's father, I will have to decide if I want to pursue finding out who is. I'll be honest. I don't think that's something I'm going to do. At least, not until she's older."

"But is that fair to Ally or to her father?" Knox asked.

Bree headed to the small sitting area where she had left her computer. "I don't know. I didn't have a choice in telling you. Not with the information I had from Brittany. And not now after I got to know that you aren't the person I thought you were. I told you about Ally as much for her sake as for yours. I promised that I would be truthful to her, and keeping this from her isn't the right thing for me to do."

She opened the laptop and began to sign in to her email account. "But I'll be honest. If you had wanted to walk away after I told you about Ally, I would have been okay with that."

He looked at her and she could already feel the crack forming on her heart. Because she knew the man Knox was now. He wouldn't walk away no matter how much more simple it would make both their lives.

"Open the email, Bree. I'm not going anywhere."

* * *

Knox sat down beside Bree as she opened the email from the lab. This was it. His life could change forever at this moment. Looking over at Bree, he had to admit to himself that his life had already changed. Bree had opened up the possibility of a new world to him. One that he hadn't known he wanted. Already he was trying to figure out how he was going to fit a little girl into his life as a traveling doctor, always moving from town to town. And every time he pictured his new life with Ally, Bree was always there, too. Right beside him. And that was just one more thing that scared him. He knew she was scared. She'd raised Ally alone for eight years and now he was there threatening the life she'd made for them.

"Okay, here it is," Bree said as she hovered over the results, her finger hesitating before tapping it.

As the email opened, Bree reached for his hand, the connection to her soothing in a way he couldn't explain. She had made it sound like the two of them were adversaries, but still, she wanted him beside her. He tightened his grip, hoping to give back some of the comfort she so readily gave to him.

They read the email silently, but together.

When they had both finished, Bree shut the laptop, then turned to him. "My sister might have had a lot of faults, but lying wasn't one of them."

Knox just nodded his head. He was so full of emotions that he couldn't speak. He had a daughter.

The sound of little bare feet slapping against the wooden floors seemed to be the only sound in the house. Bree let go of his hand and moved away just moments before Ally ran into the room, her damp hair flying around her face. She dropped down on the couch between him and Bree, the smile on her face disappearing as she looked between the two of them. "What's wrong?"

"Nothing is wrong," Bree said, before looking at Knox. "It's just as it should be."

The words struck Knox like a battering ram, opening his eyes to what was really there before him. Ally was his daughter. His daughter. Wow. His mother was going to need sedatives when she got the news.

And when was he going to tell her? It wasn't right not to share the news, but didn't Ally need to be told first? And how were they going to tell Ally? Because it had to be both of them telling her. That, he knew.

"Why don't you tell Knox good-night and go get your book out for us to read?"

"Can Dr. Knox read the book with me?" Ally asked, looking from her aunt to him. His chest was suddenly tight as emotions he'd never felt before began to surface. His little girl wanted him to read to her? Was it possible that she felt the connection between the two of them without being told? Was that even possible? The two of them had gotten along well since the moment Bree had introduced the two of them. Knox didn't know everything about Bree's life before they started working at the clinic together, but wasn't it more likely that Ally just hadn't had many men in her life? Bree was very focused on Ally and her career. It could be that like him, she hadn't had time for a serious romantic involvement, and having a man at their home was just something different.

"If he'd like to do that, it's fine with me," Bree told her niece before looking over at him.

Knox didn't miss the pool of tears that were forming in her eyes. While he'd been there processing what being Ally's father meant for him and his family, what had Bree been feeling?

"Please?" Ally asked, hopping up and down on the seat next to him.

This was the first thing his daughter had

asked of him. Looking into Ally's brilliant green eyes that reminded him so much of Bree's, he knew he couldn't disappoint her. "Sure, but you might have to help me with the big words."

"I can read most of them, but Aunt Bree has to help me sometimes. She can help you, too," Ally said, her face all serious with not a hint of a smile.

"I think the two of you will be fine without me," Bree said, giving her niece a watery smile. "And I've got some work to do on my computer before I go to bed."

Knox gave Bree a smile, unsure what else to do as Ally took his hand and began to pull him down the hall to her room. He and Bree had a lot to talk about, but it would all have to wait until Ally went to sleep.

A half an hour later, after reading a total of four pages before Ally had fallen asleep, he returned to the living room only to find her aunt with her own eyes closed, her hands resting on the keys of her laptop. Carefully, he removed the laptop before taking the seat next to her. Bree shifted and her head came to rest on his shoulder. But instead of waking, she seemed to settle into sleep even deeper, her lips curving into an innocent smile, so much like his daughter's.

Like his daughter's. Wasn't it weird how that thought seemed to come so easily now? An hour ago the thought of having a child was something foreign and frightening. Now it just felt…right.

Bree's eyes blinked open and she looked around the room, slowly sitting up. "Ally?"

"She was asleep before the wizard had his first dance at the ball," Knox said, staring down into Bree's sleep-drugged eyes.

"She'll be disappointed in the morning. It's one of her favorite scenes," she said, stretching and moving away from him. "Thank you for doing that."

"Thank you for letting me," he said. "Thank you for everything. I don't know how I can ever repay you for taking care of Ally all these years. I don't want to think about what might have happened to her if you hadn't been there for her."

When Bree stiffened beside him, he realized he had said the wrong thing. "I don't mean to insult you. I know she's your niece and you've taken care of her because you love her."

"She's not just my niece, Knox. She's my child in every way except that I didn't give birth to her. We're all the family the two of us have had. Until now," Bree said as she moved away from him, then let out a deep sigh. "I know we have a lot to discuss, but I think it would be best to wait until another day. We're both tired and there's a lot for both of us to take in now that we both know the truth."

"Bree, I don't want to make this hard on you," Knox started, then stopped. Of course this was hard on Bree. That test had changed her life, too. But not all change was bad. In his way of seeing things, this could be a good thing for both of them. He just had to give her time to see that.

Pulling her feet up onto the couch and curling into a protective ball, she looked so small and defenseless. He tried to think of something to say. It was as if all the tension that had existed between the two of them before they had begun to work together had suddenly resurfaced. They'd come so far and now it was more important than ever that they got along.

But she was right, it was late and they were both expected at the clinic the next day. Standing, he looked down at her. "We'll talk tomorrow."

"Tomorrow," Bree said, nodding her head. "We can both talk tomorrow."

CHAPTER NINE

WHILE KNOX TRIED to catch Bree between patients the next day, they were both busy from the start of the day until Lucretia put the closed sign out on the office door. Bree had mentioned earlier in the week that there were only a few days left before school was out for the summer break. He expected things would be hectic till then, but he wanted to discuss when, and how, they were going to let Ally know that he was her father. It was the *how* that worried him the most. He wasn't equipped for a "how I met your mother" type of conversation with an eight-year-old.

He'd just finished seeing his last patient of the day when Bree stepped out from the exam room with her own patient. He waited while she handed the patient a prescription along with some samples before he joined her.

"And this is Dr. Collins," Bree said, introducing him to a young woman who looked to be about Bree's age. "This is Kelly. She's just moved to town and needed a refill on her birth control until she can get set up with a primary doctor."

"It's so great that this clinic is open for walk-ins. There's nothing like this where I'm from and my insurance doesn't start for another two weeks. I've got three little ones at home. I didn't want to take a chance on adding to that number."

While Bree and Kelly discussed things from potty training to the best time to change from a bottle to a cup, Knox listened. He'd missed both of those steps with Ally. He'd missed all the firsts. First steps. First words. Even the first day of school. He couldn't blame Bree for any of that; she had only been looking out for his daughter. But still, he wished he'd been there. He was sure Bree would be glad to share baby pictures, but it wasn't the same as being there. He'd just have to make a point of being there for all the other things, though how was he going to do that? He'd spent the past few years traveling from clinic to clinic. He and Bree had a lot of things to discuss.

"Well, that's the last one," Lucretia said, locking the door behind Bree's patient. "I think we might have set a record today. I know Dr.

Reynolds will be impressed when he returns and sees the numbers. We've been able to see almost twice as many patients since you brought Bree here. Maybe he'll be able to get some other midwives in to help."

Knox had kept Dean Reynolds up-to-date with the running of the clinic through regular text messages and when he'd mentioned bringing a midwife resident in, the other doctor had thought it a great idea. Neither of them had expected it to be this successful. Knox had especially been concerned after the way Bree had initially reacted to Dr. Warner's suggestion that she spend time at the clinic.

"I'll mention it to my preceptor and my nurse counselor at the college," Bree said. "I've enjoyed the work here and I've gotten a lot of experience I wouldn't have gotten otherwise. I'm sure there are more midwives that would be interested."

"I don't guess I can talk you into staying," Lucretia said.

"I don't know what I'll be doing once I finish my residency. But if I'm in Nashville, I'll certainly try to volunteer a couple times a month," Bree said. The alarm on her watch went off, and she slid the straps of her backpack on. She was about to make her escape before they had a chance to talk.

"Do you have a moment to discuss…a few things?" Knox asked, aware that Lucretia would overhear anything that he said to Bree.

"I'm sorry, but Ally's class is having an art exhibit this afternoon at the school and I promised I would be there."

Knox was surprised at the hurt her words caused. Shouldn't he have been invited now that Bree knew for certain that he was Ally's father? He decided then and there that he wasn't going to miss another day of his daughter's life. "I'd love to see Ally's artwork. We can talk on the way there."

While Bree hesitated, Knox headed for the door. The hurt he felt from not being invited was turning into anger, something that was very rare for him. He fought against it as they exited the building as neither of them said a word. Bree's car door had barely shut when he let go of the words he had been holding back. "Why didn't you tell me Ally had something going on at school? I thought I made it clear that I wanted to be a part of her life."

"It's just a bunch of pictures drawn by a class of eight-year-olds. I didn't think you would be interested," Bree said, her eyes fixed on the windshield in front of her as she started the car.

"But it's my eight-year-old's pictures," Knox said, then realized he sounded like an eight-year-old himself.

Bree looked over at him then; her bright green eyes held none of the sparkle he was used to. "I'm sorry. I didn't think about inviting you. Like I said, it's just a bunch of pictures that they've drawn throughout the year."

"Is it a big deal to Ally?" Knox asked, knowing the answer. "I remember all the school activities that my parents missed while they were out touring. I remember the disappointment of not having anyone there for me."

"Ally isn't you, Knox. I've been to almost every activity she's had at school for the last three years." She looked at her watch, then turned off the car. "I realize this has all been a shock to you. We both have a lot to process. I promise that I'll be better at communicating with you while we work things out, but you using words like *my daughter* isn't going to help. Ally is mine, too."

"Of course, Ally is yours, too," Knox said, his hands instinctively running through his hair. He was messing all of this up with Bree. He didn't want things to be this way. Not for

Ally. And not for him and Bree, either. They both wanted what was best for Ally. They needed to be united or this could turn into one of those ugly battles adults get into over their children.

And maybe that meant giving them both some time to come to terms with what this new reality would mean for the two of them was a good idea. "I'll admit that finding out Ally is my daughter has brought up some old feelings I probably need to deal with. I know you've been there for Ally and I shouldn't compare my childhood to hers."

"How about, for now, I promise to include you in Ally's life while we sort out things between the two of us?" Bree asked. "We can enjoy today and then I think we need to deal with things between the two of us before we move forward with telling Ally anything."

"I can live with that. I think seeing us together more would be good for Ally, too. It would give her more security when we tell her about me being her father. Get her used to me being around on a regular basis. Does that work for you?" He wanted to move forward with telling Ally about him, but he understood that he and Bree had to do it together. He'd have to be patient.

And he'd enjoyed spending time with Bree and Ally before he'd even known about the possibility of being Ally's father. Now spending time with them would mean even more. He also hoped that working out things between them would also include more kisses like the one they had shared at the ranch. He had to believe that her response to him that day meant she had felt the same magnetic pull that he had felt almost from the moment he'd met her. That wasn't magically going to go away just because of the results of the paternity test.

"I can work with that," Bree said, restarting the car. "The most important thing is for us to make this as easy on Ally as possible. That means both of us taking into consideration what is best for her in whatever decisions we make."

Was she unknowingly answering Knox's thoughts about her words and the situation that they were both in now? Was that her way of telling him that they needed to ignore what had been building between them? If so, he would have to make it a point to change her mind. Because just like things would never go back to the way they were before he learned he was Ally's father, he didn't want things to go back to the way they had been before he had found Bree.

* * *

Bree watched Knox as he went from picture to picture with Ally pulling him down the line of drawings that had been hung on her classroom walls. He smiled and commented on each picture as if it were hanging in a New York City museum. It should have surprised her, and it would have two months ago when she had thought of him as a spoiled rich kid who had gone through life ruining young girls' lives, just like she had imagined that he had done to Brittany. But now that she knew him? No, it didn't surprise her at all. What did surprise her was the way her heart hammered every time he turned to look at her and gave her that wicked smile of his that sent shivers running up her spine and heat settling in places where it shouldn't be. How could she have such a response to a man whom she'd given the power to take away the child she'd raised? Shouldn't her heart see the danger it was in? Well, maybe her heart did, but her body wasn't listening to anything it had to say.

"Look, look! Those are my pictures there," Ally said, dragging Knox down to where her pictures hung. Bree recognized one of them as being the picture her niece had drawn of her family. "That's a picture of me and Aunt Bree in front of our house. And this is a picture of my mommy in heaven. My teacher helped me draw it because my friends asked me why I didn't have a mommy or daddy and I didn't know what to say."

Bree pushed back against the pain of seeing an eight-year-old's idea of what her mother would look like as an angel. Sometimes she felt very inadequate in filling her sister's place as Ally's mom. It was something she had dealt with from the first moment she'd held Ally in her arms. Mostly, she had learned to ignore the feeling that she wasn't enough. It wasn't that she wanted to replace her sister. There would always be a place in both Ally's and Bree's hearts for Brittany. But looking at the picture of a stick figure woman with hair the color of Bree's and eyes that matched hers, too, Bree could feel the loss Ally felt and she had never known how to fill it.

As if Knox understood that this was something she was sensitive about, he reached back and took her hand, pulling her up beside the two of them. Then he did something that was totally unexpected. Taking out his phone, then smiling at Ally's teacher, who had been hovering around the parents and students, he waved her over to the three of them. "Do you mind taking a picture for me?"

Ally's teacher took the phone as Knox turned Bree toward the camera while draping his arm across her shoulder and positioning Ally between the two of them. If Bree's smile was a little watery when the teacher handed the phone back to him, he didn't comment.

"This is Aunt Bree's boyfriend, Dr. Knox," Ally said, introducing him to her teacher.

"I...ah..." Bree tried to get the denial out of her lips, but the words were jumbled up inside her brain as she tried to recover from her niece's words. Looking over at Knox for help, she watched as he introduced himself and shook the woman's hand, never once denying Ally's statement. By the time Bree could form a half-witted sentence, the teacher had moved on to another student.

When Knox suggested that they stop at the same pizza place they had visited before, Ally immediately set to getting Bree to agree. It was easy for Bree to see why Ally thought of Knox as her *boyfriend*. Bree had spent more time out with Knox in the past three weeks than she'd spent with any other man since she'd had Ally.

As they ate, she watched as Ally and Knox laughed at a show on the screen above their table. She had never noticed before, but the two of them had a similar laugh. One of those whole-body laughs where their grins were wide and their eyes crinkled in the corners. She couldn't help but laugh, too, even though she wasn't watching the show. She only had eyes for the two of them as they clowned around with each other. With everything in her heart, she wished she could freeze that moment. There were so many things that would be changing soon, for all of them. But she didn't want to think about that tonight. Tonight she was going to just enjoy them being together like this. If a part of her was pretending that the three of them were just a normal family out for the night, who did that hurt?

When Knox looked over at her, his eyes shining with happiness, she picked up her glass of wine and took a sip before giving him a smile. He was a good man. An honest man. A caring man. One that worked in underprivileged communities when he could work in any OB/GYN clinic in the country. And it was already clear that he loved Ally just as much as she did. What more could she ask for as a father for her niece?

That was why after he carried the sleeping little girl into her bedroom and helped Bree get her tucked into bed for the night, she decided that he deserved some one-on-one time with his daughter.

"I've got the early-evening shift at the bar Saturday night. Would you like to watch Ally for me?" she asked as they stopped at the door.

"Of course, I'll keep Ally. What time do you want me here?" Knox said. It almost hurt Bree to see how happy her request made him. It was like giving a starving man a piece of bread. He'd been like this since the moment he'd found out Ally was his.

"If you could be here at four-thirty I can make it in by five. I'm only working till eleven. I take the early-evening shift so my usual baby-sitter isn't too late getting home. She just lives across the street, but she's older and her husband doesn't like her out any later than midnight." Bree had always thought it was more that Fran's husband couldn't sleep himself until his wife came home. Not that she minded. She knew that she had been lucky to have so many people to help her out with Ally over the years.

"I'll be here," Knox said. He opened his mouth to say something else, then stopped.

"What is it?" she asked. "If you have something else planned, it's okay."

"No. I'm not on call this weekend. There's nothing I'd rather do Saturday night."

He stepped closer to her and placed a light kiss on her lips, lingering there for only a second, resting his forehead against hers. Before she could react, he'd stepped away. "Thank you for this evening."

She watched as he made his way to where a car waited for him and she wondered what he would have said if she'd had the nerve to ask him to stay the night instead of taking a hired service back to the office to get his own car. If the look in his eyes before he'd left was any indication, she was pretty sure he would have stayed. And she would have been glad to let him.

CHAPTER TEN

KNOX LOOKED AROUND what had been Bree's orderly living room. He hadn't known what to expect, but the stack of books and pile of games that lay open around the room wasn't it. Though Ally had never appeared to be a low-energy child, she'd been more energetic than usual. Maybe it had been the ice cream he'd brought for dessert. Or the sprinkles that they'd added when Ally had shown him where her aunt hid them.

Looking at the clock, he knew he had only moments to get the mess cleaned up before Bree arrived. He didn't want to give her the impression that he couldn't handle taking care of his eight-year-old daughter. He needed her to see him as a capable parent. He had a lot to make up to both Bree and Ally. He didn't know how he was going to do it, but he would spend the rest of his life trying.

As the front door opened, he stacked the last

of the board games together. Turning, he saw
that the smiling Bree that had left just hours
ago now looked like she couldn't take another
step. The laughter that had been in her eyes
when she'd been warning Knox of all the ways
Ally would try to escape her bedtime was gone.
Her mascara was just smudges under her eyes
now and there was nothing left of the pretty
pink lipstick that he'd been thinking about
since the moment she'd walked out.

"Hard night?" he asked. He hadn't made it a
secret that he didn't like her working as much
as she was, but he knew she wouldn't appreciate his concern. He would have to be very careful when he approached the subject.

"It was bachelorette party central tonight.
There had to be at least ten of them that came
in. The place was packed," Bree said, landing
on the couch before slipping her shoes off.

Knox watched as she wiggled her toes back
and forth as if trying to return the circulation
to them. He sat down on the rug in front of
her and pulled off her simple white socks and
began to massage the pale pink polished toes.

"What are you doing?" Bree asked. He
looked up to see her eyes closed, and the mus-
cles of her tired face relaxing.

"My father used to do this for my mother

when they'd had a long night on stage. She said it helped her unwind. Is it working?"

Instead of answering, she let out a moan, then stretched her legs out farther, arching her back and burrowing into the couch. Something inside him awakened with that sound. His mind went to places he'd been avoiding since the day they'd kissed at the ranch. When she arched her back and burrowed deeper into the couch, he forced himself to concentrate on what he was doing. Then his hands moved up to the calves of her legs and the tension in her body disappeared. His hands reached the backs of her knees and he looked up to see Bree watching him, her eyelids barely opened. When she didn't tell him to stop, he continued.

Unfortunately, his own body was tightening with each stroke of his hands across her soft skin. Desire ran through his system, the heat of it flooding his veins. His heartbeat drummed to a different beat in his chest, each beat becoming faster and faster. What had started as a way to comfort Bree had turned on him. His body was now as tight as a guitar string. He didn't know when he'd ever been this aroused.

Then his hands slid higher, brushing against the tattered hem of her denim shorts, and Bree let out a gasp before arching her back again.

"Do you want me to stop?" he asked as he came up on his knees, his eyes even with hers.

"No, please don't stop," she said, her hands tentatively coming up to rest on his chest. She bit her lower lip then looked up at him, an innocence and trust in her eyes that had his body going into overdrive. Bree had always been a woman of secrets to him, always holding back something even as she smiled and laughed and looked so innocent. He wanted to know all her secrets tonight, especially the ones her body held.

He moved over her and slowly lowered himself until their lips touched. She tasted of sunshine and honey and when her tongue welcomed his, he couldn't resist the pleasure there. They tangled, released and then tangled again, his mouth wanting more and more as it caught each moan she gave him.

When her hands reached for the hem of his T-shirt, he scooped her up off the couch and carried her toward the bedroom. Her green eyes seemed to shine in the darkness as they left the light of the living room and headed down the hall. When her mouth moved up his neck, he had to stop and lean against the wall. "If you don't stop, we won't make it to your bed."

"Really," she said, surprise and a sweet, sexy smile dancing across her swollen lips before they returned to torturing him as they moved down to his collarbone.

"Behave," he said as he gritted his teeth and forced his feet to start moving again. Only the presence of his daughter in the room down the hall kept him moving forward.

He made it to the door of her room, pushed it open and unceremoniously dumped her in the middle of the bed. He finished stripping his shirt off and then paused at the sight of Bree staring at him. When she came up on her knees and put her hands on his belt buckle, his whole body went rock-hard.

"I don't know exactly how to do all this, but I think I can handle it," she said. Her hand began to undo his belt while her lips trailed soft kisses down his chest. What was she saying? That she was innocent? That couldn't be; she was only four years younger than him. He was suddenly out of his depth.

"Are you saying that you're a virgin?" he asked, his head swimming from the possibility.

Bree's hands stilled and she sat back on her heels. "Is that a problem?"

There was a vulnerability in her voice that shook loose every protective instinct in his body. "No, sweetheart, it's not a problem. It's a privilege. I just need to know. I don't want to hurt you."

"Okay," she said, her hands less sure as they fumbled with his belt now. His hands covered hers and he bent down to kiss her. The desire that had almost consumed them earlier returned as he nibbled at her lips until she was moaning again.

While this would be a first for Bree, it would also be a first for him. The women he'd been involved with before had always been as experienced as him. Even his first lover, one of his parents' crew members and a few years older, had been skilled in the art of making love. He wanted to make this special for both of them, but especially for her. He knew in his heart that this was a memory he would always treasure. He wanted to have a memory just as precious as she was.

When Bree finished removing his belt, he let her unzip his jeans, but stilled her hand when it closed around him, wrapping his around hers. Her grip tightened and he moaned as he locked her eyes onto his, his hips rocking against her hand. "This is what you do to me, Bree."

As his control began to crumble, he removed

her hands and raised them over her head. "Stay like this."

He thought she'd protest, but she kept her arms up as he peeled her T-shirt off her body, uncovering a pale pink bra that displayed softly rounded breasts. Her skin was a pale pink that reminded him of peaches and cream and he knew it would taste just as sweet. Unable to help himself, he bent and licked the top of each breast. The shiver that ran through her body, transferring itself to him... His body shaking, he held himself in check. He removed her bra, his mind taking in each curve. He laid her down and undid her shorts, while his lips sprinkled kisses over her breasts then down her abdomen. Time stood still for a moment as he spread her legs. When he looked into her eyes and saw not only desire, but trust, too, his heart filled his chest with an emotion he had never shared with another person.

"Do you know how special you are, Bree Rogers? Do you have any idea what you have done to me?" he asked.

"I just know that I want you," Bree whispered back to him. "Is that enough?"

He didn't answer her back. For now it would have to be enough. But when he bent his head and tasted her most private places, he knew that this night with Bree would never be enough for him.

Bree's mind tried to wrap around the reality of the moment while her body flooded with sensations that it had never experienced. Finding Knox waiting for her when she'd come home had seemed so right tonight. And when his hands had begun their lazy exploration of her legs as he'd massaged each aching spot, she'd been overcome with a desire for more as every nerve ending in her body called out to be touched by him. She'd arched into his touch as her body had cried out for more. Just more. But of what?

When his lips had touched her, she'd thought, *This is it. This is what I need.* But still, that hadn't been enough.

Now, as she lay there with all her innocence exposed to him, the desire for something more was almost painful. He lowered his head and gently kissed the inside of her thigh, and her body almost bucked off the bed. Never had her body been so sensitive. She bit her lip as his lips lazily moved inside her thigh. And then his hands parted her and her breath caught as his tongue raked across her center.

Her hands clutched his head, her fingers tangling in his curls, and her body came off the bed as she was suddenly inundated with sensations that wanted to overwhelm her. It felt like every nerve ending she had was too sensitive. Knox's hands joined her mouth as he left no part of her unscathed as he tormented her with a pleasure that built until she wanted to scream. She tried to tell him it was too much, but the words died in her throat as the pleasure inside her body began to build. As the orgasm hit her, she grabbed on to it, embracing it. Her world shattered and she knew everything about her had suddenly changed.

When her mind righted itself, she opened her eyes to find Knox staring down at her. With her brain still jumbled, she could only get out the most important of words. "More."

"Are you sure?" Knox asked, his face set in hard lines, his body hard against hers, his breaths coming just as fast as hers.

"Please," she said as she lifted a hand to his cheek. He wouldn't understand that she had never been with another man because there had never been one she'd wanted to share her first time with, until now. "I want this. With you."

Even as relaxed as she was, her body tightened as she watched him roll on a condom he'd produced from his jeans. He was as beautiful a man undressed as he was dressed. Uncertainty filled her, along with fear that she'd disappoint him. Of course, she knew the mechanics and she'd read enough on the subject to know what to expect.

But when he entered her, so gently, she found a new desire as he filled her. If there was pain, the pleasure overrode it. And when he began to move inside her, she let her body respond, holding nothing back from him.

As a new climax, this one even stronger than the one before, began to build inside her, she opened her eyes and found his eyes fixed on hers. A scream tore through her and his mouth sealed over hers as they both rode the orgasm out together. Yes, her world was definitely never going to be the same again.

"I have to go," Knox whispered in Bree's ear, brushing her hair aside as he applied a soft kiss to her neck.

Bree opened her eyes and saw the clock. It was almost five. Her mind tried to remember the day. Was she at the clinic or the hospital today? No. She'd worked the night before. Before…

Her eyes popped open and she took in her

surroundings. She was in her bed. The sun had begun to come up, casting shadows between the dark curtains on her windows, and she could see a pile of clothes scattered across the wooden plank floors.

She'd worked last night at the bar and when she'd come home Knox had been there. More memories of the night returned, explaining why she was in her bed and why Knox was bending over her.

She'd slept with Knox. She wouldn't regret it. It had been perfect. Knox had been perfect. Not that she was really surprised. The attraction between them, though she'd tried to ignore it, had been growing for a while.

But still, he was the father of her niece: the one person who could take her away from Bree. How would it affect Ally if she ended up involved with him? And shouldn't she feel some kind of guilt for the fact that her sister had once been, though shortly, involved with Knox? It was a complication that they didn't need in a relationship that was already complicated both emotionally and legally. It was just too bad that her body and her heart hadn't come up with that information before things had gotten this far.

There was so much between them that had to

be settled before they could address any of this. But instead of sitting up and facing all of it, she closed her eyes and pretended to fall back off to sleep. When Knox kissed her forehead before leaving, she curled deeper into the bed covers. Maybe if she buried herself deep enough, she could just this once enjoy her memories of the night before she had to face the consequences that would come with the day.

CHAPTER ELEVEN

MONDAY MORNING, Bree walked into Legacy Women's Clinic cautiously. She'd never had the experience that other women talked about as far as the awkward mornings when you saw someone you'd slept with. There'd been no walks of shame for her. While the other college girls had been hooking up with guys, she'd been raising her niece. She didn't know how to handle things like this. She didn't want to embarrass herself or Knox by making too much of the fact that they had slept together. But how did she do that when what they'd shared had been earth-shattering to her? How did she act all nonchalant when she knew just seeing him would bring up memories of the night they had shared?

When the first thing she saw was Knox where he stood deep in a conversation with Sable, the office manager, she did the first thing she could think of. She ducked into the first door she could find. It wasn't until she heard someone clearing her voice that she realized it was Lori's office. Turning, she found her mentor, along with the practice's other midwife, Sky, staring at her.

"Sorry, I just…" Bree tried to think of some excuse that would have her interrupting the two of them. Before her brain cells supplied her with anything that sounded plausible, Sky went to the door and cracked it open.

"Well, well," Sky said, shutting the door behind her and giving Bree a questioning look before looking over at Lori. "Since I'm thinking it would be very unlikely that you are trying to avoid the office manager, it seems our new midwife is avoiding Nashville's famous bad boy."

"That's not who he is anymore," Bree said, realizing too late that taking up for Knox was the last thing she should have done. "I mean, I don't think it's fair to judge him by what he did when he was a kid."

"Oh, she's got it bad, Lori," Sky said.

Bree felt the blush as it crept up her face. Bree knew she was only teasing her, but the midwife had hit too close to the truth.

"Stop teasing her, Sky. It wasn't that long ago that you were mooning around over Jared."

"I never," Sky said, then stopped. "Okay, maybe I did."

When Lori's eyes turned back to her, Bree wanted to slide under the door and take her chances with being cornered by Knox even though she still didn't know she'd feel uncomfortable seeing him there after what they'd shared. How did people do this? It wasn't that she was embarrassed that they'd had sex. Or that she felt they'd done something wrong. They were both consenting adults. It had just seemed so intimate. And he knew she had been a virgin. She'd bared so much of herself to him. Been so intimate when she normally held back so much. Maybe the word for what she felt was *shy*?

"When me and Jack set it up for you to work at the clinic, you were very adamant about not wanting to work with Knox. I think your exact words were 'I just don't find him particularly likeable.' I take it that has changed? Did the two of you kiss and make up?"

Bree's face got even hotter. There had been a time when she and her sister had teased each other unmercifully like this. She missed the closeness that she'd shared with her twin. It had been years since she'd had someone to tease her.

"Oh, my goodness, you kissed him?" Skylar said before busting out laughing.

"Sky, stop it. You're embarrassing her," Lori said before turning to Bree. "Please tell me you didn't kiss him."

When Bree didn't answer her, Lori dropped her head onto the desk. "It's all my fault. I feel like I threw you to the wolves."

"Okay, the two of you need to stop," Bree said.

"I'm sorry," Lori said, lifting her head. "We shouldn't have teased you. But in all seriousness, I don't want you to be hurt. I know Knox has changed a lot since he went into medicine. The work he does in the rural areas is tremendous. But what do you really know about him?"

Bree almost laughed. The two of them had no idea. Not that she could explain all of that to them. His being Ally's father would eventually come out. There would be no way to keep that news private. It was even possible that it would be reported in the media at some point because of his parents, which could bring up the story of Brittany's death. She and Knox would have to find a way to protect Ally from the attention if that happened. Just one more reason to make sure they told Ally about her mother and Knox carefully. The child had lost her mother suddenly; it didn't seem right that she should suddenly be faced, while unprepared, with a daddy, too.

"I'm a big girl. I can handle it," Bree told the two of them, turning toward the door. And for the first time since Knox had left her bed, she felt like she could handle it. She could handle all of it. The way her and Knox's relationship was changing, the need to find a way to explain Knox's sudden presence in his daughter's life to Ally, and even the fact that Knox could now have more rights to her niece than Bree did. Knowing him now, she felt safe that the two of them could work together to make all this work. And yes, she was even beginning to believe that she, Knox and Ally might be able to find a happy ending together.

That thought put a smile on her face that lasted throughout the day. After that, the hours went by fast as she and Lori saw mostly obstetric patients and then attended a late-afternoon delivery, which left a smiling new family with a healthy baby girl. It wasn't until she was rounding on their last postpartum patient that she saw Knox. She started toward him, then saw that he was in a deep conversation with one of the anesthesia nurses. When the woman smiled at him, Bree remembered her toothpaste-ad smile. A feeling came over Bree that she had never felt before. Possessiveness? Jealousy? A mixture of both? It wasn't a feeling she liked. While she had no claim over Knox, she also knew he wouldn't have slept with her if he was involved with someone else. That thought calmed the green-eyed monster that had wanted to come out. Instead, she managed a smile and wave as she passed the two of them in the hall, then continued to her patient's room.

She wasn't surprised when she came out to find Knox waiting for her. She'd known in her heart that he would want to see her as much as she wanted to see him. It seemed like days since she'd seen that smile of his, and seeing it made her smile, too. Why had she been so concerned that things would be awkward between them? There was no awkwardness now. Instead, there was an openness, an honesty, that had always been missing. She liked the way things were between them now better than the way things had been when she'd been keeping secrets.

"I'm glad I caught up with you. I kept missing you at the office," Knox said when he saw her. "I'd thought we'd share lunch, but you were tied up with Lori."

"It's been a busy day. Do you have a patient delivering?" she asked.

"No, I've just finished a Cesarean section. A patient with a complete previa came in bleeding," he said, falling in beside her as she started back down the hall toward the exit.

"The mom and baby?" she asked, though she knew they had to be okay or he wouldn't be standing there all relaxed.

"Both doing good, though mom is receiving her second blood transfusion now. I was going to see if you'd let me take you and Ally out to supper, but I think I'd better stay here. She's still having more bleeding than I would like. I wanted to spend some time with y'all, though."

Looking down at her watch, she saw that there was only a few minutes before her alarm would go off and she'd have to be on her way to pick Ally up at the local athletic center, which provided summer day care. "I understand. I'm about to head out to pick up Ally now. Maybe you could call later tonight?"

"I will," he said, then turned when one of the labor and delivery nurses came rushing toward him, calling his name.

"That doesn't look good. You better go. Just call me later," Bree said, waving him away when he looked back at her. She watched as

Knox jogged toward the nurse then started giving orders. She heard *OR* and knew his patient wasn't doing well. There had once been a time when she'd wanted to be the doctor standing there giving orders. Tonight she was glad that it wasn't her.

Bree rushed into the county clinic pulling a slow-moving Ally by the straps of her backpack behind her.

"There you are. I wondered if you were going to show up today. I know this is your last week but it's not the time to be slacking," Lucretia said with her usual big-dog bark and her puppy-dog bite. Then Ally peeped from behind Bree. "Wait. Who is that?"

"This is Ally, my niece," Bree said. "And Ally, this is Ms. Lucretia. She works with me and Dr. Knox."

Ally gave the woman a little wave, then looked around the room. "Don't you have a TV in your waiting room?"

"When we got to Ally's summer care program there was a note that they had a water pipe burst and would be closed till it was fixed. Knox said it was okay for me to bring Ally to work. I thought maybe she could hang out in reception with you?"

"Of course, she can. I can always use a helper," Lucretia said.

"Did I hear my name?" Knox said, coming in from the back of the office. "Hey, Ally. How do you like the clinic?"

Bree watched as Ally's disappointed face changed immediately. Running across the room, the little girl threw herself against Knox. Hugging Ally, he looked up at Bree. Even with her limited experience with it, she knew that it was love she saw in Knox's eyes. But when he looked down at Ally, Bree couldn't help but wonder if all that love had been for his daughter or if, maybe, some of it had been for her.

Which was a ridiculous thing for her to even be worrying about. Why did her mind constantly go to the negative where Knox was concerned? Was it the uncertainty of where the two stood after the night they'd spent together? Probably. She lay in the bed last night waiting for his call, the whole time wondering if she was making too much of that night. And then she'd remember how happy he'd seemed when he'd seen her at the hospital before he'd rushed off to an emergency, and she'd felt better.

But when the hours without a call from him had continued to tick away, she'd been left feeling forgotten and alone. Was this what her sister had felt like?

She realized then that Ally had been talking to her. "Can we, Aunt Bree?"

Bree looked from Ally to Knox. "I'm sorry, can we what?"

"I was telling her that my mother had invited the two of you back to the ranch this Saturday. I know it's Jared and Sky's weekend on call, so you and Lori should be free." There was something in Knox's voice that said this wasn't a simple invitation. He seemed to be holding his breath as he waited for her answer. Her mother's instinct was warning her that something was up.

"How about we talk about this later? We'll have patients coming in any minute and I want to get Ally set up with some of her toys in the reception office." Bree was prepared for the disappointment and the whining that came from Ally as she began to bargain in order to secure Bree's agreement to the trip. What she wasn't prepared for was the disappointment in Knox's eyes. But when he turned and walked away, she knew that they would be discussing this later.

But when the morning rush hit and Bree went from patient to patient performing everything from Pap smears to treating abscess infections, she didn't have the time to worry about the fact that both Ally and Knox weren't happy with her. Between every patient, she checked on Ally. While she might not have been happy with her aunt, the rest of her behavior couldn't have been better. Lucretia had put her to work stapling together the handouts they supplied to the women they see to find other resources to help with housing and food. Not for the first time Bree thought how lucky she was that she'd been able to provide for Ally over the years. It hadn't been easy, but her little girl had never gone to bed hungry and she'd always had a safe place to live.

She'd just checked on Ally and was headed back to see a new patient when Knox waved her into an empty exam room.

"Can we talk for a minute?" he asked, the seriousness in his voice so different from his usual joking manner.

"I have a patient waiting," she began.

"There will always be a patient waiting. It won't take but a moment." Knox opened the door wider and she walked in.

"I wanted to talk last night, but by the time I left the hospital it was too late." When he offered her a chair, she took it. If he wanted her to be seated, he had already decided that she wasn't going to like whatever it was he wanted to say.

"The patient with the previa? How is she?" Bree asked, mainly because she had worried about the patient when she'd left the hospital, but also so she could stall Knox from saying whatever it was that she knew would change things between them.

"There was no stopping the bleeding. I had to perform a hysterectomy," Knox said. "It was their second child and they had wanted more. I hated it, but it was either that or she was going to bleed to death. I went by to see them this morning and they both know they made the right choice."

"I'm sorry that it ended that way, but I'm glad she's okay." Of course they made the right choice. The only choice they really had. Sometimes the hardest choices are the ones where there really isn't a choice. Telling you that you have a choice is just someone's way of giving you some power over the situation, when truly your power has been taken away. Bree had faced those choices in her own life. Right now she felt that she was about to face another one of them.

"I wanted to talk to you about Ally. I think

she's ready for us to tell her that I'm her father." When Bree started to interrupt him, Knox stopped her. "Can you honestly tell me that you will ever think she's ready?"

Bree looked at Knox. She knew he was right. She'd had Ally all to herself almost from the time she was born. She knew it was selfish to want to hold on to her this way. And Knox wasn't asking for her to give Ally to him. He was just asking for her to share her niece with him. And he was right; she'd never think Ally was ready for this news. How could you prepare a little girl for something like this?

"I'm Ally's father, Bree. The longer we keep this from her, the worse it feels. She has the right to know."

"But what if she isn't ready? How do we tell her she had a daddy all this time and I didn't tell her about him?" Bree felt the tears begin to flow, but there was nothing she could do about it. "What if she hates me for keeping you from her? She's too young to understand that her mother had reasons that she thought Ally shouldn't know you.

"And what about the promise I made to my sister? I've already broke that once. I feel like I've let everyone down." Bree felt Knox's arms come around her. Laying her head on his shoulder, she spilled her last secret. "What if she grows up and realizes how much of this was because of my promise to her mother and how much of this was because I wanted to keep her all to myself?"

"It's going to be okay. We'll talk it out among the three of us. I'm not saying it's going to be easy. There's a lot that we need to figure out together. But we need to move forward, Bree." Knox moved away from her then and tipped her face up to his. "Ally loves you. Nothing that happens after this will ever change that."

Knox bent down toward her, his lips just grazing hers when a voice came from behind them. "Have the two of you forgotten that we have patients in the office? If you're going to be doing all this lovey-dovey stuff, you need to at least shut the door."

"I thought…" Knox began.

"We didn't mean to…" Bree said, then stopped when she saw the amused look on Lucretia's face. "Can you let my patient know that I'll be right there?"

"I can, but there's someone else you need to see first. That little girl, Megan. The one that those horrible human traffickers took. She's here with her mother."

Both Bree and Knox followed Lucretia out

of the room to where a young girl who barely resembled the Megan they had met sat in the waiting room. There was no trace of makeup on the young girl's face and her hair had not only been washed, but had also been cut into a neat shoulder-length bob. Her clothes were clean and she looked like she'd gained some weight. Bree was sure that there would always be trauma left from her experience, but it was easy to see that she was on a good track for recovery. Beside her sat a woman not that much older than Bree. She was pretty like her daughter, but Bree recognized the fatigue and stress in the woman's eyes. The woman had gone through hell while searching for her daughter.

"We wanted to bring you these," the woman said, standing when they entered the room. "Megan helped make them. She wanted to thank you and the police officers for everything you did for her."

"Thank you. We were glad that we could help." Bree knew that they'd only offered the girl food and a phone call, but it was those two things that had gotten the girl off the streets and back with her mother. What wrong turn Megan and her mother had made didn't matter now. All that was important right now was that they were back together. With help, hopefully the two of them would work things out and be okay.

While Knox and Megan's mother talked, Bree went to look for her own little girl. Seeing the teenager who had once been in so much danger made it seem all the more important that she hold Ally close. She knew that Knox wasn't going to take Ally and run away with her. She knew Knox would never endanger his daughter in any way. But after all the years of providing for Ally all by herself, it was hard for her to think of giving some of that control up to Knox.

When Bree found the reception office empty, she began to go through the exam rooms. When she got to the one that held her patient, the only one left in the office, she listened at the door, thinking Ally had probably gone in to talk to the woman while she waited, even though she'd been warned to stay out of the occupied rooms. But when she entered, she found that her patient was there alone. Excusing herself again, with the promise that she'd return as soon as possible, Bree went to the bathroom at the end of the hall. There were only so many places where Ally could be in the small offices. Knocking on the bathroom door, then opening it to find it empty, the panic that had begun to rise inside her burst out. "Ally? Ally? Where are you?"

Bree rushed back through each room, calling out for her little girl. When Knox met her in the hallway, she was shaking so badly that she could barely get the words out of her mouth. She had experienced this once when she and a three-year-old Ally had been shopping and the toddler had decided to hide in a clothes rack where Bree couldn't see her. There was no way to describe the fear you felt when your child was suddenly gone.

"What's wrong? Where's Ally?" Knox asked, taking Bree's shoulders and steadying her.

"She's gone. Ally is gone."

Bree's words made no sense to him. His daughter had been there just minutes before, playing with her Barbie dolls on the floor by Lucretia's chair. Leaving Bree, he rushed to the receptionist office to see the dolls lying on the floor. He started back toward the other rooms when Bree stopped him. "I've already looked everywhere. She's not there."

"What's happened?" Lucretia said, coming from the waiting room where she had gone to show Megan and her mother out.

"I can't find Ally. Was she with you?" Bree asked.

But Knox could see by the shock in Lucretia's face that she didn't know where the little girl was. "I'll call the security guard and have him start looking for her."

Knox took Bree's hand as Lucretia rushed to the office phone. "We'll start on this floor and work our way down."

"But what if she went outside? Oh, God. What if she was taken?" Bree pulled her phone out. "Lucretia, call 911. And call me or Knox if you find out anything."

Knox led Bree into the hallway, looking both ways, but seeing nothing. "She couldn't have gone very far."

"I don't understand why she would have left the office at all. We talked about this. She knows not to go anywhere without an adult. I don't even let her be outside our house without me with her."

Knox tried to think of some reason Ally would have left the office and where she would have gone. "Maybe she's just playing with us. Kids don't understand that sometimes playing like that can be dangerous."

He stopped at the first office they came to and looked around the room. "I'm sorry to interrupt, but have you seen a little girl? A blonde? Green eyes?"

"She was wearing jean shorts and a pink-and-purple plaid shirt," Bree said, her body trembling when she joined him in the doorway.

When the woman in the office shook her head, they moved on. They had visited each office on the floor, looking closely at the children in the waiting room at the county pediatric clinic. But Ally wasn't there.

They had started down the stairs when Bree's phone rang. "Hello? Ally?"

Knox tried to listen to the person on the other line but they spoke too quietly. When Bree hung up and her legs went out on her, Knox caught her and lowered her to the nearest step. Her face was paler than usual and then she began to cry.

"What is it?" Knox asked, holding Bree by the shoulders. "Tell me."

Knox had been through many tragedies in his life. He'd lost friends and loved ones. He'd held babies that had never taken a breath. He'd held the lives of patients and their babies in his hands during emergency surgeries. He'd even been in danger himself at times when he found himself up on a mountain, driving around their hairpin turns in snowstorms or torrential rains.

Nothing scared him like the look in Bree's face at that moment.

"They found her. She's in the security office downstairs," Bree said, her voice shaking with each word.

Then she lost it, there on the steps of that old, run-down county building. All Knox could do was hold on to her as the tears began to run down his face, too.

They made it to the security office as soon as they got themselves together. But when they walked in, Knox was surprised to find a solemn Ally that made no move to run to them.

"Oh, Ally, you scared me so much," Bree said, not seeming to notice that the little girl didn't hug her back. "Why did you leave the office? You know that you can't go anywhere without an adult with you."

"I don't want to talk to you," Ally said, pulling away from her.

"What? What's wrong, sweetheart? Is this about the trip to the ranch? I told you that me and Dr. Knox needed to talk about that. Being mad about that isn't a reason to run away and scare us like that."

Knox could see that Bree's fear of losing Ally was beginning to dissolve. She had moved on to wanting answers and he had an idea what those answers would be. Bending down so that he was on his daughter's level, he met her eyes. "Ally, did you listen in on a conversation between me and your aunt?"

The girl only showed the slightest hint of guilt before she put her chin up in the air. "You said that you were my daddy and Aunt Bree doesn't want me to know."

Knox heard Bree catch her breath, but he didn't look up. "Me and your aunt were having a private conversation. If you heard us say something that you didn't understand or that made you angry, you should have let us know you were there. Running off wasn't the right thing to do. You scared us badly. If you ever hear something that scares you or that you don't understand, I want you to tell one of us so we can explain it to you."

He didn't want to scold his daughter. She'd heard something that she shouldn't have overheard and she was probably as much confused as she was scared. That was on him and Bree. But he also couldn't allow her to think that running away would be the answer when she was angry or scared.

Bree bent down and joined them. "I'm sorry that you overheard us. We were both trying to find a way to tell you, but I wanted you to have some time to get to know Dr.... I wanted you to get to know your daddy before we told you. I know you have a lot of questions and we're going to try to answer them the best we can."

Ally looked from him to Bree, then back to him. "Are you really my daddy?"

Knox looked his little girl in the eye. Green eyes, so unlike his own, but still there was something in the stubborn glint of them that reminded him of his mother. "Yes, Ally. I'm really your daddy."

CHAPTER TWELVE

WHILE BREE TALKED to the police officer and the Children's Services officer, Knox took Ally over to a corner where they could talk. "Do you have any questions for me while your aunt Bree is talking to the officers?"

"Did I get her in trouble?" Ally said, biting her lip in the same cute way Bree sometimes did.

"Your aunt can take care of this. Just like she's always taken care of you."

"Does your being my daddy mean that I won't live with her anymore?"

Right when Knox thought he was prepared for anything his daughter could ask, she surprised him. He'd thought she'd have questions about how he and her mother had met. How was it that he didn't know that she was his daughter? Questions that he'd have asked. Instead, she'd asked something that was much more simple. At least it should have been. "Me and your aunt are still trying to work out the details. How do you feel about it?"

He knew these were things that he and Bree should be discussing with her together, but the choice of time and place had been taken away from them when Ally had overheard them talking.

"Don't you like Aunt Bree?" Ally asked.

"Of course, I like your aunt a lot." He wasn't about to try to explain the crazy emotions Bree made him feel to his daughter. He was still trying to understand them himself.

"Do you want to kiss her?" his daughter asked. "My friend at school, Danny, says his parents kiss because they love each other."

Knox was going to have to find out who this Danny kid was and why he was talking to his daughter about kissing. He looked over to where Bree spoke with the officers. There was nothing he'd like more than to kiss away the worried look on her face right then. "Yes, I want to kiss her."

"Then why can't we all live together?" Ally asked, her face turned up to him.

How did he explain to her how complicated adult relationships were? But did it really have to be that complicated? Wasn't the simple truth that his feelings for Bree had grown into something much more than those he should have for his daughter's aunt or for the midwife he worked with? Hadn't his fascination with her freshness, her spirit, the way she stood up to him, started long before he even knew about his daughter? Hadn't he felt something forming between the two of them the day they'd delivered the baby at the clinic when she'd smiled at him and it had suddenly felt like the two of them were the only two people in the world, and he was okay with that?

And then there was the night they'd spent together. He'd never felt so whole, so complete, as when he'd held Bree in his arms that night. It was like pieces of the puzzle that had been his life that he'd scattered recklessly had suddenly come together. He couldn't imagine his life now without his daughter. He didn't want to imagine his life without Bree beside him.

He looked down to see his daughter staring at him with such faith in her eyes. Such faith in him, trusting that he would make everything right, when all along it was Ally's innocent reasoning that pointed him toward what he had wanted since the day her aunt had accused him of having his own fan club. If he'd ever had a fan club, there was only one person he would want in it. And that was Bree.

* * *

Bree sat beside Knox as he parked his truck in front of his parents' house. Facing Gail and Charlie Collins today wasn't something that she wanted to do today, but she knew she would have to face them at some point.

"So Ms. Gail is really my grandmother?" Ally asked for the hundredth time since they'd left their house.

"She's my mother and that makes her your grandmother," Knox said once more, with a patience that he should have won an award for.

But then again, he wasn't about to face his parents while trying to explain why they had never been told about their granddaughter before now. Knox had given them the news over the phone and he said that they had taken the news well, that both of them were excited to learn that they had a grandchild even if they'd lost the first years of her life. Now it would be up to her to explain just how she had kept them from their only grandchild.

"It's going to be okay," Knox said, taking hold of her hand.

He'd been quiet most of the ride there, answering Ally's questions easily, but saying almost nothing besides that. He'd even seemed nervous when he'd arrived to pick them up. The kiss he'd given her when Ally had run to get her backpack had been little more than a peck between friends. He seemed to be somewhere else. And considering what they were about to do, she needed him to be there with her. "Are you sure they won't run me out of town the moment they see me?"

"I can almost guarantee you that by the time the day is over they will be the happiest people in the state of Tennessee," Knox said, though she noticed his eyes didn't meet hers.

Ally, tired of waiting for the adults, undid her seat belt and opened the truck door, hopping down and running toward the house before Bree could make a grab for her. By the time Bree and Knox made it to the door, Ally was already opening it and running in as if she owned the place.

"Ally, stop. You didn't even ring the bell," Bree called from behind her. The Collinses were going to think she'd raised their granddaughter as if she lived in a barn. Of course, their barn was actually nicer than the house Ally lived in.

"That's okay," an older man said as he came down the stairs. With hints of gray shooting through the same light brown hair that matched his son's, Charlie Collins had aged well. His skin was tanned and a little weather beaten, but as he walked toward them, she could see that he still had that swagger that had sent screaming women falling out into the aisles when he'd performed. His eyes were the same light gray as his son's, too. And right then he only had eyes for one person.

Ally stood staring up at him, her eyes studying him. "Dr. Knox, he's my daddy, he says that you are my grandpa. Are you okay if I call you grandpa or will it make you feel old? My friend Josie says that she doesn't call her grandmother Grannie because her grandmother says it makes her feel old. I can call you something else if you'd like me to."

Charlie Collins looked down at the little girl before he broke out in laughter as loud as if he had a mic hidden in the beard running down his chin. "I think I'd like to be called Grandpa. And what shall I call you?"

"My name is Ally. Ally Rogers. And this is my aunt Bree. You can call her Bree, though, because you're an adult."

"It's nice to meet you, Bree," Charlie said, nothing but politeness in his tone.

"It's nice to meet you, Mr. Collins."

"There she is," Gail Collins said, coming

down the stairway behind her husband. "How are you doing today, Ally?"

Ally ran up the stairs and met Gail. "I'm fine. You're my grandma."

"So I've been told," the older woman said, taking Ally's hand as she continued down to where Bree waited. "Charlie, why don't you take Ally down to the basement to see the playroom? If I remember correctly, our grand-daughter likes to play those video games you have down there."

"Can I go?" Ally asked Bree. When Bree nodded, Ally let go of her grandmother's hand and grabbed hold of Charlie's.

"I thought I'd saddle up a couple of horses for me and Bree. I'll be right back," Knox said, giving Bree an encouraging smile before head-ing back out the front door.

Bree watched him retreat, leaving her alone to face his mother. "I guess I owe you an ex-planation about why I didn't tell you about Ally when we were here."

"Let's sit down a moment," Gail said, mov-ing over to where four leather chairs faced a large fireplace. "Knox has explained most of everything, at least everything he knows."

"I've told him everything that I know my-self. I wasn't in Brittany's life at the time so

I can only say I think she had reasons for the way she handled the pregnancy. Maybe if she hadn't been killed, she would have changed her mind. I don't know."

"If it's not too painful, do you mind me asking why you and Brittany weren't communicating? Knox said you didn't even know she was pregnant until after Ally was born."

"When I look back, it was stubbornness on both of our parts. Brittany wanted a life in country music. I wanted to go to college and then medical school. She felt that my refusing to perform with her had ruined her chances of that life. I didn't think so. I still don't. Don't get me wrong, she had a beautiful voice, but there are a lot of beautiful voices in Nashville."

"I'm glad you got to go into medicine, but midwifery? That wasn't in your plan, was it? But then I'm sure raising Ally wasn't in your plan, either. You had to have considered telling Knox about her at some point. You had to know that you could have gone on to medical school if he'd taken Ally."

Knox taking Ally from her had never crossed her mind. She'd done her best to honor her sister's promise, until she'd had proof for herself that her sister was wrong. "Ally's not just my niece, Mrs. Collins. She's my child in every way. I never thought of giving her up to anyone. I did what was asked of me by my sister. Neither of us knew that within a few hours she would be dead."

"I'm sorry. I don't want to upset you. I have no doubt you did what you thought was best for Ally. I could see the love you two share when Knox first brought the two of you to the ranch. I thought then that maybe Knox had finally found someone that he could have a steady relationship with. Then I find out that it wasn't you that he was interested in, it was Ally. It's taking me a few moments to believe that."

They both stood when Knox came into the room. "Ready?"

"Yes, but is it okay if Ally stays here?" Bree asked Knox's mother. Their whole conversation was confusing to her. She couldn't tell if the woman was angry at her or if she truly was trying to figure out how all of this had taken place. And Bree had to admit, her saying that Knox was only interested in Ally had hurt, even if Knox's mother hadn't meant for it to.

"Of course. This is her home now as much as it is Knox's. Besides, I have an interior decorator arriving soon to help us make one of the rooms here just for Ally."

Not knowing what to say to that, Bree followed Knox outside. He helped her mount a sweet, gentle mare before he climbed up on his own horse. "I haven't been on a horse in a while. When I was young, me and Brittany took lessons. It's one of the few things I regret not being able to give Ally."

"I don't think you need to worry about that now. We'll make sure she gets lessons," Knox said, leading the way across a field that ran behind the house.

"Are you okay?" Bree asked. "You've been quiet all day."

"I'm fine," he said. "There's a path I want to take you up to on that hill. Then we need to talk."

His words had an ominous tone to them. What had happened since the two of them had talked last that would have made him change so much? And what had he meant when he said that *we* would make sure that Ally had riding lessons? Did he mean the two of them, together? Or was he talking about him and his parents? Anytime Knox had brought up helping Bree pay for Ally's support, she'd shut him down. She knew that at some point she'd have to accept that Knox had the right and the responsibility to help with Ally's expenses, but it was hard to take money from someone when she'd worked so hard to support the two of them on her own.

And what had his mother meant by having a room decorated for Ally? Did she think that Ally would be moving in here? Was that what Knox wanted?

And then there was the comment of his mother's about Knox being just interested in his daughter. Had he not told her that the two of them were involved? Or was that all in her own imagination? She knew that people had sex and then moved on; wasn't that what her own sister and Knox had done?

Was that it? Had she been just as naive as her sister, thinking that she and Knox were building a relationship together?

By the time they got to the top of the hill, Bree was beginning to fall apart. Had she really fallen for a man so devious that he would use her to get his daughter?

That thought stopped her in her tracks. Or in her horse's tracks. No matter what she might think, she knew that Knox Collins didn't have a devious bone in his body. If he did plan to take his daughter away from her, which she had to admit was his right as Ally's father, he would never do it backhandedly. He'd tell her gently, letting her down as easy as possible.

Yeah, he'd do something like take her on a horse ride in the country.

"Stop!" The sound of her own voice startled her as it echoed into the hills.

"What's wrong? We're almost there," Knox said.

"If you're going to tell me that you're going to take Ally away from me, I'd rather do it before we go any farther," Bree said.

Knox jumped down off his horse and came back to her. "What are you talking about?"

"I don't want you to try to sugarcoat this. Just tell me the truth. Are you going to take Ally to live with you?"

"Yes, I want Ally to live with me. That's something I wanted to talk to you about," Knox said, then reached up and pulled her out of the saddle and into his arms. "And before you start imagining the worst, though I have the feeling that you already have, maybe you should listen to me."

Bree pushed against him until he placed her down on her feet, then started up the path, leading her horse behind her. "How can I not imagine the worst when you've barely said ten words to me today and you have a mother who's right now making plans to decorate a room for Ally?"

"I haven't felt like talking because I've been trying to find a way to talk to you about this. But you've already jumped to the conclusion that I would just take the child that you have raised like a daughter away from you. Does that really sound like something I would do to you? Is that really what someone who loves you would do to you?"

Bree stopped, her horse bumping against her, making her lose her balance. Sitting there in the dirt, she looked up at Knox. 'You love me?"

"Yes, I love you. I was hoping that you loved me, too. I had this great speech I had been working on. A fancy one where after I've taken you to the top of this hill, I tell you about how all of this will be mine one day, but none of it would mean a thing if you weren't there beside me." Knox sat down beside her. "Stupid, huh?"

"Maybe a little bit. You know that I don't care about any of this stuff. I care about you and Ally. The two of you are all I need, too." Bree leaned against him then, putting her head against his shoulder. Leaning forward, she took his face in her hands and kissed him. "I love you, Knox Collins."

When they pulled apart, Knox stood and offered her a hand. "I might have brought a blanket and some wine in my saddlebags, if you want to climb up this hill with me."

Bree put out her hand, knowing that when she took his hand her whole life was about to change. "Knox Collins, nothing would make me happier than the two of us climbing this hill and every other one that life puts in front of us, together."

EPILOGUE

"Is THAT it?" Knox asked her for the third time. She'd told him when he rented the trailer that it wouldn't be big enough for everything she and Ally needed to take with them.

It had been three months since they'd told his parents that they were all moving in together. It had only been two weeks that Knox had gotten the call about a building he had been looking at to start a new clinic, one that both he and Bree could work at together now that she had passed her examinations and received all her certifications.

"Did you get Maggie's blanket?" Ally said, carrying her new puppy that her grandparents had insisted she needed if she was going to be moving away from her friends. They might just as well have bought their daughter a pony by the looks of the curly-haired dog's enormous paws.

"Her blanket and her bowls are in the back

of the truck. Why don't you climb in and get her settled." Bree helped Ally up inside the truck then turned to the friends who had come to see them off.

"I had really hoped the two of you would settle down here in Nashville," Sky told her as they hugged.

"We'll be back next month for your and Jared's wedding," Bree said, wiping at her eyes.

"And then you'll be coming back for your own wedding this Christmas," Lori said as she shared a hug with the two of them.

Bree looked down at the diamond that glittered on her finger. It was a beautiful ring, but it was the question that Ally had asked when she and Knox had shown it to her little girl that had been the brightest moment of the night. "Because you are marrying my daddy, does that mean you will be my mommy now?" It had been a night of laughter and tears, and she would remember it always.

"You ready?" Knox asked, shaking Jared's hand before climbing into the truck. Bree turned back to look at the little house where she'd worked so hard on her own to make a home for her and Ally.

But now she wasn't alone. She and Ally had Knox. They'd gone from two to three, and they were even talking about adding a fourth one to their numbers, though they hadn't shared that with Ally yet.

Climbing into the truck, she looked over at the man she loved, the one she wanted to share all her new adventures with. "Yes, I'm definitely ready."

* * * * *

If you missed the previous story in the Nashville Midwives duet, then check out

Unbuttoning the Bachelor Doc

If you enjoyed this story, check out these other great reads from Deanne Anders

A Surgeon's Christmas Baby
Flight Nurse's Florida Fairy Tale
Pregnant with the Secret Prince's Babies

All available now!